HOLD FAST THE DREAM

Lurlene McDaniel

is an imprint of
Guideposts Associates, Inc.
Carmel, NY 10512

To Mom and Dad

Forever Romances

CHAPTER 1

"ROLLING TAPE ... GOING TO BLACK ... and cue Catlin," the director intoned softly into his headset. On the floor of the studio below his glass booth, the floor director received his message. The red light flicked on at the front of the television camera and the floorman pointed directly at the auburn-haired woman in the set beneath the hot, bright lights.

She received her cue, looked straight at the camera and said in crisp, well-articulated words, "Good evening. Welcome to 'Inside', the news program that brings you today's issues today. I'm Catlin Burke and my guests this evening are the three men running for the U.S. Senate here in Massachusetts."

Catlin turned in her chair and watched as the camera pulled out to include a wide shot of the set. The three politicians glanced toward the impersonal glass eye of the camera and Catlin began her introductions.

"First, Incumbent Harold Cleaver. . . ."

The stately man with the heavy jowls and thick white hair nodded.

"Second, John Nolan, prominent attorney and former State Prosecutor. . . ."

He also nodded and smiled slightly.

"And third, Matthew Carr, political newcomer, running on the Independent ticket."

This man, too, nodded and smiled. But his was a full, warm smile that ignited his green-flecked brown eyes and caused the camera to pause a split second longer on his face.

Catlin marveled privately at his composure. He didn't display the nervous mannerisms of a newcomer to television. She had met her guests earlier, of course, in the briefing room an hour before the taping. It was standard procedure to meet with the guests prior to a program and advise them as to what to expect during the taping of a show. It helped put even the most inexperienced of them at ease. She had checked through each interviewee's background statements, discussed her basic approach, and familiarized them with the format of the show.

Naturally, she hadn't revealed all her questions. After all, this was to be a news program and she wanted to keep them alert, a little off balance, always waiting for the unexpected. It was her trademark.

"Tell me, Senator," she continued as camera number two flicked on and her face filled the monitors in the director's booth. "Amid all the uproar about suspected corruption in your office, why are you seeking a third term?" She delivered the line matter-of-factly. Though she'd warned him during the briefing that she would ask about the scandal surrounding his office, he obviously hadn't expected it to be her first question.

The senator cleared his throat and leaned slightly forward. "I will be vindicated," he said somewhat peevishly. "My enemies—" and he glanced around the set at his two opponents—"would like me to drop out of the race and concentrate on my defense. But I will not! I am not guilty and time will prove me right!"

Catlin tried not to let her own skepticism show. The evidence was already beginning to mount against Cleaver. That was why the quest for his seat had become such a wide-open race. And to have a candidate run on an Independent ticket—as was Matthew Carr—was even more rare.

She turned her attention to Carr. He intrigued her. He was born for the camera, she thought, all more than six feet of him. He was slim, but broad across his squared shoulders. He had thick straight dark brown hair, intense light brown eyes flecked with green, a square jaw accentuated by high cheekbones and a deep cleft in his chin. Yet, there was something more about the man than his obvious good looks. Something challenging and alluring within his spirit. Something that reflected a deep-seated passion for life. Something profoundly different.

"Mr. Carr, you're completely new to the world of politics. Why did you choose to run at this time? And for this office?"

The man with the tantalizing presence and the intense eyes stared directly at her. Her heart skipped slightly, beneath his unfathomable gaze. *Why doesn't he look at the camera like the others?* she wondered. *Why is he looking straight at me?*

"I'm a Christian, Miss Burke," Matthew said. "And I'm alarmed about what's happening in this country. I'm alarmed about the overt humanism that's taking over in areas the founders of this nation had originally intended for God and the Bible to dominate. When they sought to separate Church and State, they did not mean that government should abandon God. In fact, Miss Burke, the First Amendment guarantees us freedom *of* religion. Not freedom *from* religion. There's a big difference."

A mild shock wave reverberated through her. She had known in the briefing room that he was running on a "Christian" platform. The statement was clearly

9

printed on the background sheet handed to her by his campaign manager. But it was different to hear him confess it with such conviction in front of TV cameras. Politicians were supposed to be a cautious lot. Mr. Carr's remarks were not at all judicious.

"Such as?" She asked the question before she realized it. She had intended to query the third candidate before going into in-depth discussions about each man's philosophies.

"Our forefathers prayed. Out loud. In public. Most sought God's counsel before they made any decision, any policy. Today the leaders of this country seem afraid to admit it if they pray. Ashamed to say, 'I don't have an answer, but I know Someone who does. Let me consult the Bible'." Matthew smiled his disarming smile. It sent a warm surge through her body. Though she didn't know much about Christianity, she found herself wanting to believe him. Wanting to think he would pray for help if he needed it, instead of bluffing his way through as so many politicians did.

The Senator shifted uneasily in his chair and John Nolan cleared his throat. Quickly Catlin turned her attention to Nolan. She shuffled the papers in her hands, stalling for time to regain her composure. Matthew's answer had flustered her more than she cared to admit; he seemed so sincere. She wasn't used to the attribute. Not in her line of business.

"Mr. Nolan, how do you think you can serve the constituents if you're elected?"

The small, balding man with the hawk-shaped nose and thick glasses answered, "I intend to bring integrity back to the office," he said, taking an obvious dig at the incumbent. "My background and years in the judicial system have convinced me that people are sick and tired of crime. They are sick and tired of being victims. Like Mr. Carr, I think people want to return to traditional values—"

"I advocate a return to *Christian* values," interrupted Matthew Carr.

Catlin could tell that Nolan was caught off guard. She suspected he wanted to pair up with the Independent, gang up on the senator and then break away at some other time to establish himself as the most viable candidate. Carr apparently wasn't going to let him get away with it. She realized that Carr was forcing the viewers to see how each of them differed, with himself and his Christian platform as the only alternative.

Clever she thought. Aloud she asked, "There's a difference?"

"A big difference," Matthew affirmed. "Tradition serves man and his interests. It's simply another form of humanism."

Nolan bristled. Catlin smiled inwardly. Matthew Carr was in firm control of the show. But she was a journalist, and she was after the truth. "Tradition has served you well, Mr. Carr. You're clearly the wealthiest of the candidates. Traditional money earned in traditional ways."

It was true. Matthew Carr's banking empire and other business interests made him one of the richest men in the state. She didn't know much about the Bible, but she had always thought of Christians as humble, poor people who lived good moral lives and kept pretty much to themselves.

"Yes," Matthew agreed, his eyes never leaving her face. "I am a very wealthy man. It's been God's blessing and, I might add, never a point of corruption in my life."

"How do you figure that?" she fired back.

He smiled broadly. "Well, since I don't need it, why would anyone offer me money for favors? I can't be bought, Miss Burke."

From the corner of her eye, Catlin could see the senator squirm in his chair as a slow flush crept up his neck and across his face. *Touché!* she thought. Matthew Carr had pinned him and there was absolute-

11

ly nothing he could say in his defense. She eyed Carr with renewed respect. He was sharp. Very sharp.

The rest of the interview moved along briskly. The senator tried to skirt questions about his legal hassles and concentrate on his ". . . long record of service to the people of Massachusetts." Nolan kept returning to his "law and order" position. Matthew re-emphasized his Christian principles. Catlin was surprised. It was obvious that he didn't care whom he alienated. He was out to rally Christians. Rally them to vote, choose, take a stand for their beliefs. He was outspoken, yet so totally charming that she believed he just might do it.

When the floor director finally gave her the hand signal to wrap up the show, Catlin felt amazement. The hour had gone so quickly. More quickly than she ever remembered. She made her farewell remarks into the camera, waited until the red light blinked off, and heard the director announce into the studio, "Okay, Cat . . . that's a wrap!"

She stood, stretched and turned to thank her guests. Nolan and the senator nodded curtly, joined their aides and left the studio immediately. Matthew Carr did not. "Thank you for having me on the show," he told her, his bright eyes boring through her.

Catlin dropped her own gaze and shuffled script papers. Why did the man unnerve her so? She spoke a bit brusquely, trying to concentrate on her routine and not on the charming man standing in front of her. "And we thank *you*, Mr. Carr. I trust this exposure will aid your campaign."

"The people *do* need a choice," he said quietly.

She looked at him then. His gaze was open, direct, and challenging. She knew she should confront him. Any good reporter would. But he wasn't quite like anybody else she had met—even with her extensive contacts. He *believed* . . . really believed in what he was doing. It showed in his eyes. In his face. In his

12

voice. She backed down and smiled almost shyly at him. "Perhaps we'll meet again on the campaign trail," she said. "It's only April. A long time till Election Day in November. . . ."

He nodded. "I hope we do meet again. And I hope it's very soon." He scanned her face boldly. Normally, such close scrutiny would have made her bristle. She was used to male attention. And she was very adept at keeping men at arm's length. But there was no untoward suggestion or innuendo in his gaze.

Catlin's pulse quickened. She felt oddly disjointed and off-balance with him. She set down her script and reached for her briefcase, but a sudden rush of cold night air from the outside studio door sent the papers flying out of her grasp.

"Oh!" she cried, snatching at the swirling papers.

"Shut the door, Louis!" the floor director yelled.

"Sorry, Miss Burke!" he apologized.

Catlin, Louis, the floor director and Matthew Carr grabbed at the wayward papers, gathering them together. As Mr. Carr handed her his share of the booty, their hands brushed, causing a sharp snap of static electricity. When she gasped and took an involuntary step backward, Carr instantly withdrew his hand.

"Excuse me. I didn't mean to shock you."

Her eyes met his and a slow blush crept into her cheeks. He smiled, a slow and intriguing smile, and said softly, ". . . Until the next time," then turned, joined his aide at the studio door and walked out.

Catlin stood for a full minute, staring into space, at the place where she had last seen Matthew Carr. "Fool!" she snapped to herself impatiently. She gathered up the rest of her materials and shook her head, hoping to erase the last clinging vestiges of his presence.

Matthew Carr is just a man running for office, she told herself. *A politician . . . like all the others . . . out*

13

for Number One. But the electricity that had sparked between them was more than a natural phenomenon. She knew that instinctively. And it troubled her.

Catlin slipped into her private dressing room, kicked off her shoes and flopped onto the bench in front of her dressing mirror. She was exhausted. It was after ten o'clock. She had spent twelve hours at the station, and all she felt like doing was going home to a nice hot bath.

But she couldn't leave yet. Not until Taylor called. She stared long and hard at the private phone next to her make-up tray, willing it to ring. She knew he would summon her soon, as he did at the end of every work day, to view and discuss the "Inside" interviews. After all, Taylor Shentell wanted his station, his news team, his investigation in the forefront of the impending election fray. And Catlin felt a deep obligation to give him what he wanted.

There was no doubt that it was Taylor's belief in her that had put her where she was today—at the forefront of the news department of Channel WTSB. She looked vacantly into the mirror and let her thoughts drift. . . .

Catlin Burke had long ago acknowledged that she had more than her share of physical beauty. It was an accident of birth; merely the way the genes aligned on the DNA spiral. A blessing—and a curse.

When she was a small child, people had stopped her on the street to marvel at her extraordinarily beautiful auburn ringlets and honey-colored eyes. "Look," they would say, "how unusual! Her eyes are gold! Would you just look at that!"

Later, in school, she had quickly become a favorite with teachers and classmates alike. They couldn't help being drawn to her. But Catlin grew uncomfortable with the constant attention. She began to notice that her looks caused people to catalog her differently

14

from others, without waiting to discover that, beneath the flawless exterior, there was also a keen intellect.

Catlin had been a brilliant student. Always at the top of her class. Always earning scholastic honors. Everything came easily—grades, friends, opportunities. She understood that and almost came to expect it. Except that it often galled her that the world considered her beauty first; her academic achievement, second. It began to frustrate and confuse her.

Throughout her college days, she had tried to downplay her beauty. She went to great lengths to conceal her fine-boned features, arching eyebrows, thick shiny auburn hair and lithe, slim body. She did not wear make-up, nor did she go in for trendy fashion. She redoubled her study efforts. She earned scholarships. She made Honor Rolls, Dean's Lists . . . and, in her senior year, was chosen Homecoming Queen.

When it came time to go out and face the business world, Catlin made some revolutionary changes. By then, she'd learned there was no use to hide her beauty. So, she made an uneasy truce with the two warring factions within—a peaceful co-existence pact between her beauty and her intelligence. She decided to make them work *for* her. For the total presentation of the final product. For the success and advancement of Catlin Burke. In short, her beauty opened doors, and her intelligence kept them open.

Therefore, it was no surprise to anyone, not even to Catlin herself, that at twenty-five, she was nearing the top of the heap in the world of broadcast journalism. In the Boston marketplace, she was already a household word, viewed on the evening news by a large and adoring audience. She was network material and everybody knew it.

Her work was exceptional. Her reports probing and incisive. Her exposés, tough and uncompromising. Her presence on the small screen riveted viewers. She had an easy, natural style of delivery. A gentle, yet honest and appealing quality that gave her credibility with her viewers. She was, in short, dedicated to journalistic truth, yet never lost her ability to touch the human heart. She demanded the best of herself. And she gave the best she had.

But the climb to the top had cost her. She was aware that her natural self-assurance made her seem too perfect . . . flawless . . . even unapproachable, and that many of her colleagues referred to her as "The Ice Princess." The appellation only amused her.

She was aware, too, that Taylor Shentell had chosen and personally groomed her to dominate the Greater Boston television news market. And no accident that, in the process, he had fallen in love with her.

The jarring ring of her telephone snapped Catlin out of her reverie. She picked up the receiver at once. Taylor's low voice came over the wire.

"Cat? I'm ready for you. Master Control brought over the tape. I've skimmed it once. Now I want to go over it with you. There are some things we need to discuss. . . ."

"Be right there," she said and hung up, her curiosity piqued. Taylor often watched the actual taping from inside the director's booth; not so this time. For this taping he had secluded himself in his office, content to view it afterward on his private monitor with Catlin at his side.

She brushed her long hair and arranged it on her shoulders, slipped on lizard skin pumps and tossed an ivory-colored linen jacket over her apricot silk blouse.

She took the back way to Taylor's private office. Through the dark bowels of the now silent studios, booths and tiled halls, passing through the quiet coolness of Master Control, where two engineers sat at massive consoles monitoring the mechanical spinning of tape machines, film projectors and slide chains.

Opening a massive door, she entered the plush, carpeted world of the WTSB executive suite. The overhead lighting had been dimmed, and she passed silent business offices that, during daylight hours, made the other side of the station hum. The building was like one large symbiotic creature—the offices, typewriters, telephones of the business side feeding the cables, consoles, cameras and sets of the studio side. Together they worked to one end: To put pictures into hundreds of homes all over Boston. Television. The industry never ceased to intrigue her.

She rapped softly on the inner door of Taylor's sanctuary and he admitted her with a smile. "Hi, beautiful. I've missed you."

He caught her hands in his and pulled her gently to him. She leaned against his chest for a few minutes, savoring the warmth of him, allowing him to stroke her hair and rest his chin absently on the top of her head.

Taylor was both handsome and dynamic, a big man with piercing blue eyes and black hair peppered liberally with gray. Catlin had always thought the silver strands lent him a look of maturity, self-confidence, and authority. It was an accurate image. At thirty-eight Taylor Shentell ran one of the most successful television stations in Boston. He fascinated her, and she still felt somewhat awed by the knowledge that he loved her. He could have had any woman he wanted. But for some reason, he wanted Catlin Burke.

"Can I get you something to drink?" he asked, breaking the spell of intimacy.

"A Coke?" She crossed the room to sit on the burgundy, velour-covered sofa.

"You got it." Taylor stepped to his private glass-topped bar, dropped ice cubes into frosted glasses and poured Coke over hers. "I want to talk about this interview. I think I smell a story."

Joining her on the sofa, he leaned over his video cassette machine and punched the forward button. Catlin watched her own image jump onto the monitor screen set into the oak-paneled wall. Taylor fast-forwarded the tape, then paused when the image of Matthew Carr appeared on the screen. She leaned forward slightly. She hadn't been mistaken during the taping. Matthew Carr was both articulate and adroit.

Taylor made his way through the entire tape in that manner. Fast forward. Stop. View Carr's segments. Stop. Fast forward. He was clearly concentrating on the one man. At the end of the tape, he rewound the cassette and turned to Catlin.

"Well—" he ventured settling back into the sofa's cushions and looking straight at her— "what do you think?"

She chose her words carefully. "Matthew Carr certainly seems sincere. I'm not sure the voters will go for his 'Christian' platform, but I have to admire his courage for speaking out so openly about his convictions. Personally, though, I don't think he has much of a chance of getting elected."

"Do you view him as a man of principle?"

She shrugged. "Sure. But then, aren't they all? Just so long as it's their 'principles'?"

"I disagree," he told her. "No . . . men of 'principle'," he fairly spat the word, "tend to make me very nervous. I find them highly suspect. It's men like Carr who turn into fanatics—"

"Oh, he hardly seems like a fanatic," Catlin interrupted.

Taylor shot her a warning look. A look that dared her not to challenge his suppositions. She broke off, knowing better than to push him, but she was irritated that he had the power to control—even a woman of her fortitude—with a single glance.

"You're new to Boston, Cat," Taylor continued, pacing now. "Oh, you've got a lot of savvy. You've

18

picked up on the politics here, know the area 'movers and shakers.' But you've got a lot yet to learn.''

As usual, his words were right on target. But his delivery rankled, leaving her feeling slightly hostile. It was true. Taylor had brought her into his station only four years before, had opened doors for her, allowing her to mingle and deal with important dignitaries and public figures on the strength of his connections. She owed him a great deal.

But it was also true that she had worked diligently to earn the respect of the public. It was not Taylor alone who was responsible for her current position as top anchor and investigative reporter.

Still . . .

"What do you want me to do, Taylor?" Her tone was cautious.

"I'm assigning you to the Carr campaign for the duration of the election.''

"What?!" she cried, leaping to her feet. "You can't be serious! I have a hundred irons in the fire right now. What about the Police Department corruption story? I want to do that story, Taylor. It's mine! Besides,'' she sought frantically for a rebuttal, a defense to keep from bending to his unreasonable demand, "Carr's not the story. The senator . . . he's the *story!*''

Taylor turned his back, unwilling to face her, his hands thrust deep into the pockets of his impeccably tailored suit. "Everyone's going after the senator, Cat. Cleaver's through.''

. "You don't know that. He hasn't even been investigated yet. It's all in the preliminary stages.''

"I'm telling you, he's through.'' His tone of voice warned her to back off. "No, the real story is Matthew Carr. . . .'' Taylor continued his restless pacing. "A man like Carr. Rich. Powerful. A member of the social register. Now he suddenly wants to run for office on a 'Christian' platform. Why?''

"He believes in it!" Catlin blurted.

Taylor paused and stared, with alarming lack of compassion, straight into her eyes. "Come on, Catlin," he chided. "Where's your objectivity? Christian platforms are hot. It's just a ruse."

Somehow his words offended her. She had an innate sense of news—she knew that, and Taylor ought to know it, too. Taylor's skepticism about Carr did not match her own feelings about the man. Still . . . Taylor was right about one thing. She was fairly new in the marketplace. Perhaps there was more to the story than was immediately evident.

She sighed deeply, feeling drained and tired—too tired to fight about it now. Taylor was still the boss. Regardless of his personal feelings for her, she was his employee, obliged to give him loyalty.

"What about my other assignments?"

"We'll talk about that tomorrow," he said. He crossed the floor and once again grasped her hands. "Cat, listen to me. I know what I'm doing. I think Carr is out to dupe and deceive the people. As a newsman . . . as a citizen, I can't let that happen. You're the best I've got. I want you to expose him."

She looked deeply into his icy blue eyes. "And what if he's for real? What if he's everything he says he is?"

Taylor dropped her hands and turned away abruptly. "Then report that," he said tersely. He picked up some papers from his desk top. "In the meantime, I want you to dig. Get everything you can on him. Get his permission to tag along on his campaign. He'll probably jump at the chance for so much exposure. You can have the news van and any two crewmen you want to work with you.

"Naturally, I want you to keep your six o'clock anchor and 'Inside,' he added hastily, sensing her distress. "But the investigative stuff . . . get rid of it. From now on, your first news priority is Matthew Carr. Understood?"

20

She knew it would be useless to argue. And in a way, she didn't want to. Certainly, Taylor's style angered her. And she hated to leave her other assignments. But she, too, wanted to discover the "real" Matthew Carr. She felt the familiar stirrings of analytical curiosity. Who was this man who walked with equal confidence along the corridors of financial power and the path of Fundamentalist Christianity?

"All right," she agreed quietly. "But, Taylor, please know one thing."

He tilted his head and waited for her to continue.

"I will report what I find. Good . . . bad . . . corrupt or blameless. I will report the truth about Matthew Carr."

He gave her an indolent smile. "That's why I hired you," he teased, assuming once again the role of doting mentor. "And that's also the reason I love you." Then he pulled her into his arms and kissed her longingly on the mouth.

CHAPTER 2

"SO THAT MEANS I'll be taking over those assignments?" The question came across the conference table from Ken Anderson, WTSB co-anchor and News Director.

Catlin set down her coffee cup and checked the "Carr Project" off her agenda sheet. The early morning staff meeting had been moving along swiftly until she had brought up her new task. Ken eyed her suspiciously and Catlin ignored his gaze. It was always that way between them. He—jealous of every move, every assignment, every promotion she received. She—trying to remain professional and objective.

In a way, she didn't blame him. Before her appearance at WTSB, Ken had been top dog, absolute reigning monarch over the station's news department, answering only to Taylor. Then Catlin had come on board—a woman, handpicked by the boss—unseating him as six o'clock news anchor. Scooping the hot stories. Threatening all that he had worked for during his journalistic career. Ken was still News Director, but it was a hollow title. He was a figurehead, and everybody at the station knew it.

Catlin, sensitive to his feelings, had tried to assume a role of underling. But it had been no use. Ken never felt comfortable around her. He was always suspicious and hostile. Finally, she had given up.

"That's right," she confirmed crisply. "Mr. Shentell wants me to cover the Carr campaign. I'll be traveling a lot, following him around. I'll be too busy to concentrate on much else. I'll still do news anchor and 'Inside' when I'm in town. But for now, I'm to delegate all other responsibilities."

A low buzz among the staff members seated around the conference table followed her announcement. It was a highly unorthodox move—even for Taylor Shentell. As a UHF channel, WTSB didn't have to answer to a network hierarchy. Taylor was sole owner and manager of the station, and he was legend in the industry for his bold and reckless management. He had proved to have an uncanny instinct for the business.

Fresh out of college with a degree in broadcasting, Taylor had acquired the failing television facility over fifteen years before. Somehow he had persuaded investors, the bank and the FCC that he was the man to build the fledgling station into a voice in the Boston marketplace. And he did, by investing in new equipment, new personnel, and assuming an aggressive marketing posture.

When Cable hit the airwaves, and network affiliates lost their exclusive rights to programming, Taylor took advantage of the break in their iron hold. He jockeyed and scrambled to position his station into one of dominance through market research and a dedication to ". . . giving the people what they want." He succeeded. One by one, he bought out his investors. Now, Channel 48 was his alone, and he ruled it with a cunning that sometimes bordered on ruthlessness.

In recent years, he'd sunk a lot of money and time into the local TV news market. It was simply something he wanted—to be Number One in the news ratings race. Every time the Arbitron rating books came out, he moved closer and closer to his goal, inching up rating point by rating point. And Catlin Burke was one of the top reasons for the success of WTSB News.

Catlin marked off the last item on her agenda and broke up the meeting. "Maggie," she called to a tall frizzy-haired woman, while the newsroom staff filed out the door and back to their duties, "stay here a minute. I need to talk to you."

Maggie Collins paused. Ken lingered also. But once he realized Catlin wasn't going to confide in him, he stalked out of the room in a dark humor.

"What do ya need, boss lady?" Maggie asked in her gravelly voice.

Catlin smiled. "Research." She liked Maggie, a tough-minded woman in her fifties who had spent all her life around TV newsrooms. She was one of the best fact-finders in the business, with a sharp instinct for news, backed by an equally sharp tongue.

Maggie flipped open her notebook. "Carr?"

"Everything you can find out," Catlin confirmed. "Who, what, how . . . the works."

"Strange thing for the boss-man to do . . ." Maggie said absently, reflecting Catlin's own thoughts that, with manpower at a premium, yanking her off her regular duties to pursue one story for several months seemed like a waste.

Catlin shrugged. "I told him that. But you know Taylor. . . ."

Maggie gave her a half-smile. "Who argues with success? Not Maggie Collins. That man's never played by the rules. And look where he is today."

"Anyway, get right on it. I'm going to call Carr later today and try to set up an interview with him.

Also, break the news to him that I plan to keep him in the public spotlight for the remainder of the campaign."

Maggie nodded. "I'll do what I can."

"Do you know anything about him? I mean, you've been in the Boston marketplace a lot longer than I."

"Something *is* rolling around in my brain," Maggie said in her scratchy voice. "But let me check it out first. I do know he's rich. And if votes were for sale, he could win by buying all he wanted. Seems to me he's some sort of 'blue-blood,' too. But let me do some checking."

Catlin nodded and walked thoughtfully back to her office. The whole thing puzzled her. But she also felt a mounting excitement about seeing Matthew again. Would the electricity still be there between them? She half smiled, remembering the look on his face when their hands had touched. And her heart raced slightly at the memory.

She scheduled the interview, through Carr's press aide, for Friday morning at his home which was simply referred to as "The Van Cleef-Carr Estate," a vast and well-attended mansion set back in the Blue Hills. She knew nothing about the place. But, like everyone else in the city, Catlin was aware that it was a landmark of other times, other social orders, other dreams. In a city steeped in American history, the great Van Cleef-Carr mansion was a beacon, lighting a tunnel to the past. Catlin itched to go there and check it out.

At the buzz of her office telephone, she looked up from her list of interview questions and reached for the receiver.

"Hi, beautiful." It was Taylor's familiar voice. "Time out for lunch?"

She glanced at her wall clock. Where had the morning gone? "Love to," she told him. "Your office?"

25

"Veal scaloppine."

"I'm on my way."

Taylor was a strange combination, Catlin thought. Brusquely efficient in business affairs. Debonair and impeccably ordered in his personal life. In fact, he often sought life's finer things with a vengeance. He was a gourmet, rarely going out for meals, but keeping a chef on full-time at both the station and his penthouse condominium.

He was a connoisseur of the arts, buying paintings, rare books and supporting live theater, opera, the symphony, the ballet. He was a Renaissance man, in love with tradition and all the trappings of civilization and refinement.

Yet he'd come up hard. Raised in the tough streets of Southside Boston, one of five children in a blue-collar world, he had made it on his own—fighting, scrambling, scratching, and surviving by his wits and his instincts. And he had made it big. He had transcended his other world and he would never go back. Never. Now, everything in his present existence seemed geared to forgetting that other life.

Catlin still didn't know quite where she fit into his plans. But the woman in her knew he needed her. For all his toughness, for all his education, for all his veneer of culture, he needed the softness, the tenderness, the sense of completion she brought to his life. He'd never married, although his name had been linked with some of the most fashionable and glamorous women on the East Coast.

He kissed her warmly when she arrived and pulled out her chair in the private dining area off his main office. One glass inner wall overlooked the brick-walled garden he maintained at WTSB. Tree branches, still bare from winter, shimmered with the first green lace of spring.

The tantalizing aroma of the veal and sauce aroused her tastebuds. "I'm starved! Thanks for the invitation."

They ate in a comfortable silence, each enjoying the savory food for different reasons.

"How's your project coming," he asked almost casually. But she could tell by the way he cocked his head, waiting for her answer, that he was *very* interested in her answer.

"Maggie's digging in the archives for me. I have an interview at Carr's home Friday morning."

"Good!" Taylor beamed her a full smile.

"The—uh—the staff all thinks this assignment is a little bizarre," she added cautiously, not sure of his reaction.

But he was in a good humor. He laughed openly. "When we scoop every station, every newspaper in Boston, they'll think I was crafty and clever."

It troubled her. He was so *sure* Matthew Carr would crumble under close scrutiny. She wanted to please Taylor, but not at the expense of destroying another human being. Was it the man, Carr, he disliked? Or the thing he stood for—Christianity? She didn't know.

"Come here," Taylor said softly across the table.

She reached over and took his hand. He stood and pulled her up after him, taking her face in his hands and looked into her golden eyes. "You are so beautiful. . . ."

She received his mouth tenderly. She did love him. In an odd, protective way. In a grateful, fond way. He did *not*, however, stir great passion in her. She told herself that it didn't matter. There was so much more to loving someone than "passion." She returned his kiss as warmly as she could.

Finally she drew back. "We're still on work hours," she whispered, trying to keep her voice light—not censuring, not rejecting.

He broke off, hugged her tightly. "I love you, Cat. I couldn't stand to lose you. . . ."

"You can't lose me," she chided softly. "I'm here to stay. Promise."

"Dinner tonight?" he asked as she turned to leave. She curtsied. "Yes m' lord."

He laughed. "Off with you, wench. Back to your duties."

She left his office, walking briskly through the thick pile carpeting, back to her own office. It pricked at her conscience that she didn't love Taylor Shentell the way he wanted. But she didn't.

Catlin drove through the winding streets of Cambridge almost by rote. The April air was still cool. Banks of slush lined the streets and sidewalks. But the unmistakable signs of spring—new life, new beginnings—were everywhere.

She left the narrow roadways of the city and wound upward into the exclusive Chestnut Hill area toward the Carr home. She cracked the window of the WTSB newscar and inhaled the sweet, loamy smell of fresh black earth. Behind iron fences and granite walls, tulip beds burst with colorful wax-like flowers. Overhead, delicate green buds laced tree branches, promising soon a reemergence of beauty and color and life.

Spring. It filled her with a sense of longing. Of a tender yearning for . . . what? She never knew. Yet, when the land began greening, and the just-washed smell of awakening things came to her on the breeze, she was filled with paradoxical feelings of expectant joy and wistful loneliness.

She slowed the car and crawled up to the top of a steep private roadway. At the crest of the hill, she halted in front of an eight-foot stone wall, linked by iron gates. A small bronze plaque attached to the gate read: "Van Cleef-Carr." Her heart raced with anticipation. She felt ridiculously eager to see Matthew Carr again, strangely drawn to talk to him, to know him.

She announced herself into the receiver attached to the gate, and the iron bars swung open. Entering, she

28

drove slowly up the tree-lined, winding driveway. She had heard stories about such grand estates, but nothing had prepared her for the actual sight.

In summer, the house would be obscured by the silent sentry of trees that guarded its quarter-mile driveway. But now, the house—stately, sprawling, majestic—could be seen through the barren tree branches. Catlin drove cautiously, unable to take her eyes off the grand and brooding mansion.

Its design was Georgian, classical and contemporary, thrusting red brick and wood into the bright blue April sky. It had been retouched by many architects, each adding a new façade, each imprinting it with some unique touch of bygone eras. It was the past. It was memories of grand ballrooms, powdered wigs, hoop-skirted satins and laces; a daguerreotype preserved in a timeless antique frame. It was yesterday, long ago, history . . . perfectly maintained, perfectly preserved for this, a less gentle time, a more complex age. Catlin was enthralled.

She stopped the car at the crest of the driveway, exited and walked up onto the veranda. The bell sounded melodious when she rang it. Matthew himself opened the oversized door, and his smile drew her back into the twentieth century.

"Come in, Miss Burke," he invited and swept her into the large marbled foyer of the old house. He was dressed casually, in tan slacks, a dark navy polo shirt and burgundy V-necked sweater. Relaxed and at home on his own turf, he was even more handsome than she remembered.

"Please," she said, "call me Catlin."

"Only if you will call me Matthew," he nodded.

Catlin didn't look around, content for now with merely sensing the size of the house, its cavernous foyer, its vaulted ceiling. Off to the right, however, in her line of vision, a blue-carpeted stairway led to yet another floor.

"Thank you for meeting me here instead of down at campaign headquarters," he told her. "It's really so much less congested and private. I thought it would be easier to talk without calls and interruptions."

"Believe me," she said sincerely, "I appreciate the opportunity to come here. I–I don't think I've ever seen a place quite like this." She let her eyes travel quickly around the foyer, absorbing the subtle beauty of worn marble, polished wood and a gleaming crystal chandelier high overhead.

"If you like, I'll give you a tour after we talk. But for now, let's go into my study," He took her by the arm and led her through a doorway. "It's more homey in there. It's where I live in this old place anyway."

They passed through a formal living area, decorated with heavy Victorian pieces and a fireplace with a wooden mantel. This room, at least, seemed scaled for normal people. In the foyer, she'd felt dwarfed and undersized.

From the living room, she was escorted into a library, a book-lined room, paneled in dark oak. Matthew must have been working at the massive desk, she observed, for it was littered with papers, books, and files. At one end of the room was a sitting area, furnished with a corduroy-covered sofa and a small round dining table on which someone had placed an exquisite porcelain tea service.

With a flourish, Catlin was seated at the table. "Cup of English tea?" Matthew inquired.

"In this bastion of Americana?" she asked in mock horror.

He laughed, a quick easy laugh that encouraged a smile by its very sound.

"Don't tell the ancestors," he pleaded. "They went to such lengths to dump it all in the harbor."

The room closed about her in warm contentment. It was so much friendlier than the rest of the house. From her seat at the table, she could see, through a large bay window, a hillside sloping down to meet a swiftly running brook.

She was suddenly aware of Matthew's eyes on her. Quick color stained her cheeks, and she fumbled awkwardly for her briefcase and her cassette recorder. "Shall we get right down to business?" she asked in as businesslike a tone as she could muster.

"I'm surprised you're planning to follow my campaign in such great detail," Matthew mused. "Usually the press doesn't jump on the bandwagon for someone like me. I'm new to the game of politics and, at this point, probably not perceived as much of a threat to Cleaver."

She couldn't say, "My boss thinks you're a hoax. He's sent me to expose you." She did say, "WTSB wants to follow the entire election process for our viewers. Your campaign . . . your platform is probably the most unusual to come along in years. May I deal with you directly? I mean, I'd like to avoid as much formality with aides and press types as possible. I promise not to monopolize your time, but I would like to have direct access to you."

His eyes assessed her boldly and the corners of his mouth turned up in an amused half-smile. She squirmed, imagining herself a specimen under a microscope when he looked at her like that, as if he were looking into her mind and reading her thoughts.

"You may have 'direct access'," he said quoting her stilted phrasing.

They both broke out in laughter and suddenly, she felt totally at ease with him. No longer like a reporter doing a job. More like a friend talking to another friend.

She tasted the tea. Its flavor was rich and deep, and it warmed her. "What about your business?" she asked on a more professional note. "How can you take this much time out to run for office?"

"It'll keep. I've spent years hiring competent

people just so I could set aside these few months strictly for campaigning. I don't intend to do anything else except meet the people all across the state . . . get as much exposure as I can."

Privately, she compared his attitude to that of Taylor Shentell. Taylor would never relax the reins of power he held over WTSB, regardless of his competent staff. He had to be in on every decision, every policy, every minute detail of his business.

She inhaled deeply and posed her first significant question. "Would you tell me about your Christian platform?"

He clasped his hands behind his head and stretched out his long, lean body in his chair. "Catlin," he countered, "do you know what the American Dream is?"

"You mean the stuff our forefathers talked about, or what it's become since then?"

"The *real* Dream. . . ."

"Freedom, liberty, the pursuit of happiness . . ." she defined.

"Yes . . . but based on the Word of God. Did you know that our Constitution never addresses the issue of separation of Church and State?"

She didn't.

"That idea first occurs in the writings of Thomas Jefferson—years *after* the constitution was ratified. In reality, the men who framed the Constitution never meant for Church and State to be separate. They did want to avoid a "State Church," but their first loyalty was to God." He leaned forward in his chair and pinned her with his sparkling eyes. "Do you know why the Pilgrims came to this country in the first place?"

"To worship the way they wanted to," she replied, mentally resurrecting old history lessons.

"Right again . . ." he agreed tentatively. "But there's more. The first settlers actually planned this

32

country to be 'one nation under God.' They wanted to establish America as a new Israel, a nation filled with covenant people, obedient to God and in total community with one another.''

"You're kidding." She'd never read anything like that in her history books. In fact, historians usually went out of their way to ridicule the Puritans as stoic, unyielding, unbending religious fanatics. "What happened?"

"The nature of man 'happened'," he told her with a disarming smile. "Man felt he could do it all on his own. He didn't need God. But in times of peril and genuine distress, this nation turned back to God. The earliest citizens prayed for deliverance, prayed for divine guidance and providence . . ."

Her eyes studied his face and she felt hypnotized by the power of his words, the simplicity of his message. Could it be true? Could an entire country be saved by depending entirely on God?

"If you win," she asked carefully, "what do you think you can do to turn the nation around?"

"For one thing, I intend to influence and change ungodly legislation. Someone has to hold the Legislature accountable for what it is doing." He paused and the very air seemed charged with the passion of his vision, the clarity of his dream. "So," he shrugged, breaking the spell. "That's basically why I'm running. Someone has to stand up for God. Someone has to represent His perspective."

"You want to defend God—in politics?" She attempted to sum up all that he had told her.

"I want to defend the *honor* of God," he stated. And his light brown eyes, flecked with pinpoints of green, glowed with excitement and fervor.

Catlin caught the zeal in his voice. She'd never known anyone like him. He had everything the world considered a mark of success. Yet the life force within him, the thing that motivated and drove him was like

33

nothing she'd ever encountered. He had shown her a vision, a dream—and it overwhelmed her. She also knew that if he could communicate his vision and his passion to the voters, he would become a Senator from the State of Massachusetts in November.

She probed for more information about his political ambitions. They certainly seemed legitimate enough. Surely, no one could fault him for sincerity. He talked in quiet tones, telling her about the time, two years before, when he'd felt called into God's kingdom, specifically into the arena of politics. How he'd started in local churches with his message of turning back to God, and gone into bigger churches, then civic clubs and finally into the campaign for public office.

"I know my opponents don't consider me a threat," Matthew confided, "but, Catlin, people *are* listening to me. People are scared, and they're looking for direction and answers for their lives."

"And you think God has those answers?"

"I *know* He has!" Matthew said with urgency, leaning forward.

She responded by leveling her gaze at him, her pulse quickening and her own excitement mounting. Was he right? Did God have answers for the country? For the people? For Catlin Burke? They sat for a few moments in silence, each musing over private thoughts. From far away, Catlin heard the chiming of a clock. It struck twelve times. She'd been with Matthew for two hours. It seemed like only minutes.

He, too, heard the clock. "I've kept you too long." He stood and stretched.

"Not at all," she assured him. "It was one of the most fascinating interviews I've ever had. . . ."

He took her hand and gently raised her to her feet. For a moment, time seemed to stop. She gazed at him, losing herself in the velvet pool of his scrutiny. Her mind toyed with the inevitable. What would it be like to have him hold her?

34

He spoke in soft tones, his voice coming from far away. "It was my pleasure. . . ." Then the mood lightened. "How about that tour I promised? Do you have time to go through this old barn with me?"

The spell was broken. Catlin quickly agreed. "I'd like that. I've always liked Early American lore and craftsmanship. You know—hand-made quilts, furniture, metalwork—the real thing. I've collected a few pieces since I've lived in Boston. Nothing too grand . . . just some old furniture I've been restoring in my spare time."

"Follow me." He led her through a door off the library, entering directly into a large bricked kitchen.

"Wow!" Catlin gasped, surveying the vast area. It was a blend of the ultra-modern—two ovens, a microwave, a counter filled with electric appliances—and the past—a stone fireplace, a walk-in pantry, authentic cast iron cooking utensils.

"The cook comes in at four o'clock," he said. "I'm not here much, so I use the microwave for emergency meals. See this fireplace?" He walked over to the old stone hearth. "It was in the original cabin that Philip Newton built back in 1622."

She ran her hand across the aged gray stone. "Newton. . . ." The name was new to her. She filed it away mentally. She'd check it out with Maggie when she got back to the station.

He continued, "The cabin originally stood down by the Charles River, where the Newtons had a trading post. As more and more settlers came over from England, the family began to feel crowded, so they migrated up to these hills back in the 1700s—after the Revolutionary War.

"That's when the foundations of this house were laid. It was renovated and enlarged right after the Civil War. You can tell by the outside that more than one architect has taken a crack at it." He paused. "Some Victorian chap added all those exterior gables and gingerbread," he finished with a half-laugh.

"I think it's rather quaint."

He grimaced, "I think it's gruesome. Come on, let me show you the rest." He took her through the kitchen into a Colonial- style dining room. The hand-rubbed maple table gleamed in softened light from the long windows that looked out onto the veranda. Voile curtains diffused and muted the bright noonday sun, giving the room a shimmering effect. A massive maple credenza held pewter dishes, sterling silver bowls and tea services, and copper serving pieces. Brass sconces along the walls were the only means of lighting the room at night.

Catlin imagined the room in readiness for an evening meal, glowing and waiting, the table set with lace and linen, bone china and heavy hand-wrought silver. The past, seeming almost palpable, beckoned and called to her from every corner of the quiet room.

"Of course, you've seen the 'parlor'," Matthew said, using the old-fashioned word to describe the Victorian sitting room. They entered it and walked through to the end with the formal fireplace. Hand-painted tile surrounded and set it off. A massive wooden mantel, as if struck from a single, mighty tree, stretched across the top of it. An antique clock, its face trimmed in inlaid gold, chimed the half-hour.

"So parts of this house are hundreds of years old . . ." Catlin mused aloud.

"And parts . . . like the addition on the back . . . are only ten years old." He seemed momentarily lost in thought. "I've often thought of turning it into a museum."

"Oh, you don't really mean that!" She was surprised he could even consider parting with it.

"I'm just a guardian." His words were cryptic. "Besides, the Historical Society would love to get its hands on this place."

"You mean have tourists trekking through?" Her tone assumed a mixture of distaste and horror. "How awful!"

He laughed. "It's just an old mausoleum. And it costs a fortune to maintain. Why, I don't think the wiring's been replaced in this place since they switched from gaslights." By now they were standing back in the foyer, at the foot of the spacious staircase. "And," he added, his eyes twinkling at her response, ". . . it's one hundred percent American. The marble is from Massachusetts quarries, the woods from American forests, the stone from the rivers and fields of New England. Not an imported item in it!"

"Except the English tea."

He laughed and raised his hands in mock surrender.

Catlin ran her hand along the oiled and polished banister, her eyes again traveling upward toward the second floor of the great house. The carpeted stairs were wide and inviting. About fifteen steps led to a large landing, where they stopped, curved right, then proceeded upward to the next floor. At the landing, however, the sweep of her vision was halted by a massive portrait, hanging on the wall of the landing.

The painting was enormous—at least ten feet high—framed in an elaborate gilded wood frame and pictured a woman dressed in contemporary fashion. She stood, captured forever on canvas, against the fireplace of the formal parlor.

Mesmerized, Catlin climbed the stairs, uninvited, lured by the haunting presence of the woman in the pale blue satin ball gown. She was not beautiful in the modern sense. But she was elegant, classic, reminiscent of nobility and breeding. Her hair, piled atop her head was a pale wheat color, her eyes the blue of cornflowers.

Her face, almost translucent, held a look of aloofness. Her mouth harbored a partial smile. Her eyes, so sad, belied the smile on her lips. Her hands were clasped primly in the folds of the gown that fell floor-length from bared, ivory shoulders. A large blue sapphire ring, surrounded by diamonds, twinkled on her left hand.

Catlin could not tear her eyes away from the painting. It was so life-like, so real. She expected the woman to move at any moment. Or at least nod slightly in her direction. She was vaguely aware that Matthew now stood next to her on the landing. "She's lovely . . ." Catlin whispered. "Who is she?"

He did not answer. Catlin pulled her eyes from the portrait and asked again. "Who is she?"

Matthew's face was a mask. His eyes clouded, and the muscles tightened in his jaw. "That's Sandra," he said simply, "my wife."

CHAPTER 3

IF MATTHEW HAD STRUCK HER PHYSICALLY it could not have had more impact than those two words. *My wife!* Confused, Catlin mentally sorted through his composite file, his background statement, his information packet. Nowhere had there been any mention of a wife. If it were true, why would he have left out such an important fact? No politician could hide something like that. And no "Christian" candidate could hope to avoid scandal if he were separated or divorced.

Her thought processes took micro-seconds. Her eyes narrowed as she perused him suspiciously. "I didn't know you were married. . . ."

Matthew stood looking up at the painting for a long moment. Then he turned to her and said crisply, "She's dead."

His second pronouncement was almost as unsettling as the first. "Dead?" Catlin queried, her journalistic interest piquing.

"She died six years ago." His eyes had grown guarded and cool. "But she has nothing to do with this election . . . this campaign. Catlin," he said, "I will not discuss Sandra. Not ever. Please don't ask. She has nothing to do with the here and now. I'm asking you to please respect my privacy on this one topic.'' The tone of finality in his voice closed off all avenues of discussion for her.

"Very well," she agreed verbally. But her mind rolled over his words and his subject with vivid interest.

Catlin followed him out of the foyer and onto the spacious veranda. The day, so bright and sunny before noon, had now grown bleak. Gray banks of clouds had blown over the sun, leaving the landscape looking dismal and dull. It might be April, Catlin thought ruefully, but it was still a long time before spring.

She got into her news car and turned slowly out of the driveway, knowing she had to get back to the station to sort out her work load and her thoughts. Her last sight of Matthew was through her rear view mirror. He was standing on the bricked steps of the old mansion, his hands thrust into his pockets, his collar turned up against the rising wind. "Who are you, Matthew Carr?" she asked aloud in the empty automobile.

When he had spoken to her about God and his own political ambitions, he had sounded so sincere. But now—a wife he refused to discuss? A mysterious past? Maybe Taylor was right, after all.

"Do you want this report delivered orally or in written form?" Maggie asked Catlin in her gruff, gravelly voice.

"Both," Catlin said tersely, shutting the door of her office and pulling out a chair for Maggie.

"It's not complete. But then you said get all I could, so I did." She tossed the folder onto Catlin's desk. "This is all I could get in two days," she added dryly.

The corners of Catlin's mouth turned up in a brief smile. She picked up the file and leafed through it. The tab read: Matthew Carr. She had only four hours until air time for the six o'clock news, and she knew she should be going over the reporter's agendas and concentrating on the evening's news program. But she couldn't just yet. She wanted to hear what Maggie had gathered so far on Matthew.

"Coffee?"

Maggie nodded and Catlin poured them each a cup from the coffeemaker in her office. Then she leaned back in her desk chair, leveled her golden eyes at Maggie and said, "So let's have it."

"Well . . ." Maggie began, "Carr earned his fortune by virtue of the Holy State of Matrimony. He married Sandra Newton Van Cleef twelve years ago. Met her at college where she was a spoiled little princess, and he a business major and football hero."

"I know about his academic credentials," Catlin interrupted. "What about these Newton-Van Cleefs?"

Maggie picked up the file and turned a few pages. "Right, boss lady. . . . According to local history, the Pilgrims all but tripped over Philip Newton getting off the Mayflower."

"In other words, the Newtons were some of our very first Americans," Catlin stated, amused by Maggie's delivery.

"Yankees through and through. Left England to get away from religious persecution . . . you know, all that religious freedom stuff."

Catlin nodded. She had just spent all morning listening to Matthew talk about the "religious freedom stuff." And she was inclined to agree with him. Most people had forgotten, or maybe had never bothered to find out, just what America was all about.

"Anyway, they survived the rough early years, set up a trading post at Boston Harbor, reproduced a couple of generations of Newtons and fought for ". . . truth, justice, and the American Way," Maggie intoned.

"They fought in the Revolutionary War, the War of 1812 and the Civil War. Eustis Newton moved his brood up to the hills, hoping to get away from civilization. Some of the Newtons were more sociable than others," Maggie added, peering over her half-frame glasses at Catlin as she talked.

"Actually, a *lot* more sociable," she continued. "It seems that when the new wave of immigrants came over at the turn of the century, one of the three remaining daughters—Cale Newton was the only one of the bunch not to sire any sons—got herself 'involved' with one of the new breed. One Erich Van Cleef to be exact." Maggie added hastily, "He did the right thing by her, however. He married her."

Catlin suppressed a laugh. Maggie was having a great time with the assignment, and her natural instinct for news was reflected in the thoroughness of her report.

"Van Cleef brought new blood into the Newton line, and, it seems, an uncanny knack for making a buck. He sold the family business, invested in textiles, made a mint and then sold that and went into banking.

"But he was a clever old bird, with a tough sense of Yankee independence and ingenuity. When the stock market crashed and the bubble burst in '29, he had most of his capital tied up overseas. In munitions." Maggie flashed a wicked grin. "He barely felt a ripple when the American Dream fell apart at its seams for the rest of the country.

"He channeled his interests into banking and investments and that's where the money now sits. Big money. Big influence. Charles Van Cleef inherited everything from his father, and Matthew married Charles's only child, Sandra. When she died . . . well,

42

he got it all." Maggie wrapped up her narrative with a conspiratorial smile. "Nice and neat."

"Question," Catlin's brow puckered. "They were social register types, right?"

"Their blood runs blue, if you get my meaning. They wintered in Palm Beach when it was fashionable. They have a second house on Cape Cod. The DAR claims them as their own. The list goes on and on."

"Yet Carr doesn't seem too much into that scene. . . ."

Maggie shrugged. "Not since his wife died. He still donates heavily to various organizations and is on the boards of certain historical and philanthropic groups. You know, social do-gooder types."

Catlin knew. She had suffered through many a boring interview with dowagers intent on beautifying, rectifying and restoring certain Boston areas suffering from crumbling brownstones and urban blight.

"That's it in a nutshell," Maggie said, standing. "I'll leave the report with you. I still have more to dig up on Carr's personal life. His roots and origins. This church stand he takes. His business practices. I'll get it all, don't worry."

"I never worry when you're on the trail, Maggie," Catlin smiled. But there was another, more pressing, question on her mind. "Maggie," she asked as the older woman was halfway out her door, "just off-hand . . . do you happen to remember how Sandra died?" She wanted the question to sound nonchalant and merely an extension of the interview. But her own pulse raced as she anticipated the answer. She couldn't get the image of Sandra's portrait out of her mind. Nor of the wraith-like look in her blue eyes.

"Car wreck," Maggie said firmly. "She was driving and hit a stone wall. Died on impact."

Catlin buried herself in a deluge of work and prepared for the evening news program. Ken approached her on a couple of stories, asking if he could deliver them. She agreed to all of his requests. It seemed important to him to have as much air time as she. Ken's ego was the simplest of her problems.

After the news show, Catlin did not linger in the studio. She headed straight home, longing for a nice hot bath and an evening alone. She got as far as the hot bath.

Just as she curled up on her sofa, her doorbell chimed. "What now?" she moaned, tossing her book aside and hugging her emerald-green velour robe tightly to herself. Usually the doorman notified her whenever she had company.

"Who is it?" she called through the door.

"Prince Charming. I've come to rescue Cinderella and take her out for a night on the town."

Quickly she unbolted her door and opened it. Taylor leaned in, kissed her lightly on the tip of her nose, and ordered, "Get dressed. We have reservations at ten at 'The Four Seasons'." He was dressed in a dark suit. His hair shone silver in the artificial lighting.

She stood staring at him for a moment before finally gasping, "Taylor! 'The Four Seasons' is in New York!"

He grinned mischievously. "I know. Our plane leaves Logan Airport in an hour. So stop standing there, staring at me like I'm nuts. Get dressed."

He never asks, she thought. *Only demands. Like a summons to appear in court.* It was annoyingly typical of him. But the idea intrigued her: Jetting off to New York for dinner . . . and he looked so eager and handsome, so intent on pleasing her.

She flashed him a wide and delighted smile. "Give me twenty minutes!" she called over her shoulder, already heading to her bedroom to change.

New York City! Taylor Shentell certainly had style.

They made their plane with but minutes to spare. Catlin felt a bit like a child at Christmas. Everything looked exciting and wonderful and new. Taylor held her hand and kissed her. He was delighting her and she felt sure he knew it. She responded by snuggling close against his shoulder during the plane trip and cab ride to the famous restaurant.

She wished she had had more time to prepare for the occasion. She had chosen a champagne-colored silk sheath that draped over one shoulder and left the other bare. Her hair, brushed and burnished, fell in soft cascades to her shoulders. Her coat, a satin evening wrap, was more for decoration than warmth. But when they followed the maitre d' to their table in the restaurant, heads turned.

They sat near the beautiful reflecting pool, amid banked masses of azaleas and clusters of live birch trees. The bar area was unusually large, adorned with a Picasso-designed theater curtain and an abstract sculpture of brass rods dipped in gold. Intricate tapestries lined the walls.

The meal, the service, the atmosphere dazzled her. Taylor ordered from the extensive menu . . . food with exotic French names, salads prepared at their table, desserts that flamed and tasted sweet and wonderful. He seemed to be watching her every move, drinking in her comments, her excitement, her pleasure. She stored away the memories of the evening, absorbing as much of the glitter and mood as she could.

She and Taylor complemented each other. She knew it. If only she felt the passion for him he did for her . . . She forced herself to concentrate on the food and her surroundings. She *did* love him, in her way. She *did*. To prove it, she flashed him a smile of pure delight as he caressed her with his eyes.

Afterward, he took her to several trendy nightspots, one after another. Catlin had never been to such places. She surveyed the premises, the people, the music with her detached journalistic attitude and a kind of macabre fascination.

Everything was too loud. The colors too harsh. The people too garish . . . hedonistic, pleasure-seeking, flamboyant. Yet, she watched the writhing, twisting bodies—sensuous, suggestive, startling—and wondered what their lives were like. Wondered what things drove them and what appetites they quenched with their frenzied movements.

"You're not enjoying this?" Taylor leaned over their tiny table and shouted above the roar of the pounding, pulsating music into her ear.

She wrinkled her nose and shook her head.

"Neither am I!" he shouted again. "Let's go!"

She hesitated. An hour before, she had watched him slip the doorman a one hundred dollar bill to allow them entrance. A long line of brightly dressed people clustered outside, some waiting to get inside, some waiting to catch a glimpse of the rich and famous who came to "see" and "be seen."

"Come on," he urged again and, taking her arm, led her through the press of people into the darkness outside. The cold, crisp night cleared her head and refreshed her spirits. "That's not for you, is it?"

Catlin shook her thick hair and breathed in deeply, filling her lungs with the freshness of the air.

"Nor for me," he confessed. "But I thought you might like seeing how the beautiful people live."

Catlin had told Taylor about her Midwestern upbringing. In fact, he had "discovered" her while she was hosting an early morning news show at a local station in her hometown in Ohio—her first job fresh out of college. His plane had been forced into a layover due to bad weather, and Taylor had watched Catlin on a TV set in the airport. Struck by her beauty and fresh approach to reporting the news, he had hailed a cab and gone straight to the station where she worked. Two hours later, she had agreed to accept a position with WTSB in Boston. Her career had soared ever since.

"It's only five A.M. We still have things to do," he said, taking her hand.

"Five in the morning?" she asked, shocked. "When are we going home?"

"Relax. Today's Saturday. You have the rest of the weekend to recover. Our flight doesn't leave 'til noon. We can still have breakfast and get in a couple hours of shopping before we go back."

She was beginning to feel sleepy and, though she didn't want to complain, she had put in a hard week's work.

"How about a ride through Central Park?" he asked, sensing her languid mood.

"In one of those Hansom cabs?" A sense of new adventure buoyed her spirits.

Taylor hailed a cab. Soon they arrived at the park where he hired a horse-drawn cab. They snuggled together under a lap blanket and rode through the quiet park in the predawn chill.

Overhead, the sky was streaked with the first promise of morning. Subtle grays and pinks gave way to bright reds and oranges. Catlin watched the horizon brighten through the silhouetted shapes of bare tree branches. It was going to be a glorious spring day. She could feel it. She could smell it.

She snuggled closer to Taylor, enjoying his warm masculine scent, the comfort of his broad chest. He stroked her hair. Had it been this way for Matthew and Sandra? The question floated through her mind, unbidden and unwelcome. They could have afforded to have all these things together. Did they? The image of his face—the square-cut jaw, the dancing green-flecked eyes, his quick and easy smile—drifted across her memory like a thread on a shiny sewing needle.

Why was she thinking of Matthew Carr now? With Taylor so near? Yet, she was. She recalled again how Matthew had spoken about his commitment to God, his calling, his destiny. And what was hers? To dine and dance and ride on life's merry-go-round, observing life? Reporting about life?

"What are you thinking about so hard?" Taylor's voice interrupted her thoughts.

She felt a flare of guilt. "I sit still for a minute," she confessed, "and I start thinking of work." It was a half-truth. Matthew *was* part of her work.

"How is our project coming?" They both knew automatically which project he was asking about.

"I'm not sure . . ." she mused, pulling back and looking up at his face. He was shrouded in shadow, but she sensed the tension in his face and body. "But, Taylor, so far all I have is questions about Matthew Carr. After my interview with him . . . well . . . I just don't know. He really believes he's doing God's will for his life."

Taylor hissed sarcastically. "Don't fall for it. I'm convinced he's out for himself."

"But why, Taylor? What's he got to gain?"

"Power, of course."

"He already has power." She knew it was true. Somehow, Matthew had great power. And not just social clout and prestige. He had another kind of power—the kind Taylor would never understand, and she was only beginning to glimpse. She sighed and snuggled against him again.

"He was married once, you know . . ." she added distractedly. "There's something there. I'm not sure what. But something. . . ." Again waves of drowsiness swept over her. The gentle swaying of the carriage, the steady rhythmic clopping of the horse's hooves, the softness of Taylor's cashmere coat against her cheek, lulled her into peaceful oblivion.

From far away she heard Taylor whisper her name.

48

He continued to stroke her hair and he pressed her forehead tenderly with his lips. "I love you, Cat. . . ."

"I love you, too, Taylor. . . ." she mumbled before slipping into sleep.

Monday dawned dark and threatening. It was depressing. The weekend had been so bright and beautiful. Now, it seemed as if it might snow before the day was through. At least Catlin had recovered from her weekend in New York with Taylor. She had spent most of Sunday sleeping.

At the station, following the newsroom staff meeting, Catlin organized her desk. She sorted through a stack of memos and put them in order of priority. Her phone line buzzed and she picked it up quickly. "Yes?"

Maggie's coarse voice came over the wire. "It's me, boss lady. Since Carr will be hitting the campaign trail next month for a trip through the state, want me to reserve space on the Press bus for you and a crew?"

Catlin's heart thumped. The campaign trail. She had had one brief experience at her former station, and then only as a tag-along for the head anchor. She still had mixed emotions about it. Parts of it had been exciting—the exhilaration and electricity that surrounded any political figure meeting the people. But parts had been dull and tedious—long waits with little to do, endless riding, much idle time. And, of course, there was the usual assortment of journalists smelling out a story.

Some were tired, bored and cynical, biding their time and fortifying themselves at bars along the journey. Others were hot-shots, intent on making their personnel miserable with their self-centered demands. Others were eager beavers, getting in the way, making a nuisance of themselves. And the old-timers, the veterans of such trips, had little tolerance for anyone.

She'd been told once by one elderly and slightly seedy reporter, "Politicians are a ruthless lot, little lady. They have an intense love/hate relationship with the press that borders on mania. They really hate us, you know. But they need us. And if you cross them, they'll find a way to get even. Most of these 'candidates', " his voice had taken on an edge of bitterness, "are not real smart. But they are cunning. And for the most part, shrewd and vindictive. Watch out." She had never forgotten his words. What would Matthew's campaign trail be like? She wondered.

"Yes," Catlin said in response to Maggie's question. "I'd like to take Red McIvers to run the backpack camera and maybe Sue Davis as tech. Clear their schedules for me, okay?"

"That's all?"

"The fewer, the better. Get the details for me on how long we'll be gone, the itinerary . . . you know . . . the usual."

"Give me a few hours."

After she hung up, Catlin sat musing at her desk. It was about time she touched base with Matthew again. But this time she wanted to meet him at his campaign headquarters. She needed to meet his staff, get acquainted with his representatives. And this time, it would be strictly business. She couldn't afford to be surrounded by the soft, sheltered beauty of his world. She wanted him on her own turf—the tough, demanding world of TV lights, probing questions, and honest answers. She was going to discover the real Matthew Carr once and for all.

Matthew's Boston campaign headquarters were located in a storefront in Cambridge, near the Harvard campus. Catlin learned that he had another in Springfield. A state-wide campaign took tremendous effort and coordination by a great many people. Some positions paid money to the holder, but most were handled by volunteers.

She arrived at his Cambridge base of operations, unannounced and unexpected. Four people sat at one table, stuffing campaign literature into envelopes. Two more were making phone calls. Three of them were young, looking fresh and scrubbed; three, elderly with white hair and an air of congeniality.

"Can I help you?" Catlin recognized the man at once as the manager Matthew had brought with him the night of the taping. A look of recognition crossed his face and he broke out into a smile. "Why, Miss Burke!" he exclaimed, offering her his handshake. "Hey, everybody . . ." he called to the people in the room. "Come meet Catlin Burke."

She nodded, smiled and shook their hands, accepting their compliments on her news show. One wide-eyed teen-aged girl with brown hair and brown eyes, seemed smitten with Catlin. "You're even prettier in person than on TV!"

"Yes, she is, isn't she?" The voice was Matthew's and it came from a small office door on the other side of the room. Catlin felt his eyes on her and blushed. "Welcome," he said and crossed to her side.

Standing next to him, she felt petite and feminine. His pale blue, oxford-style dress shirt was open at the collar, emphasizing his broad and well-muscled shoulders. The sleeves were rolled up to his elbows and she noted the sinewy muscles of his forearms. *Of course,* she reminded herself. *He played football.* He obviously still kept himself in good physical shape.

"You've met a few of my volunteers," he said. "And you already know Neal Wilson, my manager. My press agent, Dodd Brighton, is out right now. You can meet him later. Come to my office and let's talk."

She followed him and he pulled out a chair for her in front of his cluttered desk. "I'm preparing a speech," he explained with a smile and waved his hand over the messy desk. "It's good to see you again," he told her, a look of admiration clearly stamped on his face. Her heart quickened a little, just as it always did whenever he smiled at her. She was attracted to him. There was no doubt about that. But she couldn't let her attraction get in the way of her objectivity.

"Excuse my bad manners—dropping in on you unannounced," she said quickly, easing her slight tension in his presence. "But I'd like some information for tonight's news . . . something to help build up to this whistle stop tour you're planning."

"Then you'll be coming?" The look of interest he gave her was evident. "I'm glad," he said. "That way, I can see you every day."

She steeled herself not to respond to him. Was it just idle flattery? Did he really want to see her often? She cleared her throat. "Let's talk some more about the origins of this grass-roots movement of yours." She flipped open her notebook. "If we talk now, I can bring a crew back this afternoon and do a stand-up in the other room. You know, show your volunteers, get the flavor of the hustle and bustle. I'll quote what you tell me now, insert my own remarks, edit it all and get it on the air by six o'clock."

He clasped his hands in back of his head and pushed back in his chair, stretching out his legs. It was a position she had grown accustomed to seeing him assume when they were working.

"As I told you before, I started two years ago. In one church after another—study classes, special meetings of elders and ministers. I went to business men's prayer breakfasts, ministerial conferences, church suppers . . . anywhere I could talk to groups of Christians. I can't get elected without their support," he confessed.

"Anyway, they began to accept me, trust me. A

52

signature petition put me on the ballot as an Independent. A plurality in November will give me the office. A lot of people are counting on me, Catlin . . . donating money, time, energy. . . ."

"Big business?"

"Would it surprise you to know that many big businesses are run by Christian businessmen?"

"Favors?" she tossed out.

His eyes clouded momentarily. "I promise them nothing but a biblical stand and representation in the legislature," he said with finality.

"Narrow path to walk. Everybody expects something in return. Look at what's happened to Cleaver."

"Cleaver made his bed," Matthew said strongly. "He sold out."

"Do you really think you can unseat him?" She scrutinized his handsome face for false piety.

"My campaign, my life, are in the hands of God. My destiny is under the Lordship of Jesus Christ. I'll win if He wills it."

She eyed him curiously and once again felt the stirrings of something within her own spirit. The Lordship of Jesus Christ. She didn't know what it meant, but it evoked such fire and passion in Matthew Carr that she knew it must be awesome.

Suddenly he leaned toward her and asked, "I want to talk to you longer. But I've got a meeting and speech to give at two o'clock. How about talking some more over lunch?"

His question caught her off guard and she stammered, "I–I . . . well . . . all right."

"Good!" He beamed and standing up, took her by her hand and pulled her around his desk.

For a heart-stopping moment she was so close that she could see deep into his intense brown eyes, and smell the clean scent of his lime after-shave. Her heart hammered. His mouth, poised so close to the top of her head, caused her to arch upward. His nearness filled her senses. Purposely, she pushed away from him, dropped her eyes and turned for the door.

She had wanted him to kiss her. What was wrong with her? She was a reporter doing a job—supposedly coolly professional and emotionally detached. She chastised herself angrily and swore that she would not get so near him again.

He took her to a small café-style restaurant—an Italian place, located under the pavement a short block from his headquarters. They descended the steps into the dimly lit dining room, and sat together in the intimate silence of a private booth. Catlin munched on a breadstick and Matthew ordered antipasto and linguine with clam sauce for both of them.

"Who are your workers?" she asked, struggling to keep the meal on a businesslike basis, despite its intimate setting.

"Neal's a friend since college. A Christian, too. So's Dodd. He and his wife, May, have a background in Public Relations. They've really been a big help. Mostly because they're friends first. Everyone close to me in this campaign is a committed Christian.

"The rest, kids from various church youth groups, some from the colleges, are both idealistic and enthusiastic. It's refreshing to have them around. Without the volunteers, I'd never get anything accomplished."

"You ready for this tour?"

He gave her a lop-sided grin. "As ready as I'll ever be. I plan two more before the election in November. I wish you could come on all of them," he added with a sparkle in his eyes.

She averted her gaze. "It must cost a lot, accommodating all the press."

Traditionally the candidate paid for the bus housing the press, food, facilities, tape and film freight on their stories. She knew that his personal finances could

54

cover all his campaign expenses. But there were laws that prohibited excessive personal spending. He was like any other candidate running for any public office. His financial backing must come from a broad base of donations.

He waved his hand, dismissing the cost factors. "You know," he began as the waiter set their salads in front of them, "so far, all you've done is ask me questions. I think you owe me a few answers."

She flushed slightly.

"What about Catlin Burke?" he asked. "What does she believe in?"

"I–I'm not sure what you mean."

"God. Where is He in *your* life?"

She hadn't expected that question. Most people wanted background information—where she came from, how she got into TV—not about her religious beliefs.

She started slowly. "Don't think I haven't thought about it ever since I met you. I have. The answer is: I don't know. My parents were very upstanding, middle-class people, who took me to church. I went to Sunday school, youth groups, even Christian camp once. But that was all so long ago . . ." her voice trailed as the memories flashed like slow-motion pictures in her mind.

"I–I remember longing passionately to see Jesus when I was a child. And I seem to recall loving Him devoutly—then. But—" the pictures speeded up— "time slipped up on me. I grew up. Got interested in college, dating, my career." She shrugged. "I don't know where that devotion went. And in all honesty, I've never met a Christian like you. Christians in my youth were all so—" she groped for a word—"well . . . restrained. Self-contained. Hardly vocal and outspoken about their relationship with God."

Excitement kindled behind his light brown eyes. She didn't understand why, but she could feel his

55

genuine interest in her every word. "Catlin—" when he spoke her name, it sent a shiver up her back— "this next Sunday is Easter."

Ashamed, she realized she had forgotten that the most important and dramatic day in Christianity was less than a week away.

"I'm planning a get-together after church services for my staff, personal friends and long-time supporters. It's a barbecue/campaign kick-off/Easter celebration rolled into one up at the estate. Please come." His eyes glowed in the softened light of the room.

She felt hypnotically drawn to them, to the warmth and tenderness in his voice. "Not as a reporter," he added, "but as a friend. Come and meet the good people I've been telling you about."

She wanted to go very much. She wanted to be a part of his world again. A part of his life. "I–I'd like that . . ." she whispered.

"Come to church with me, too," he urged. "I would very much like to share this special day with you."

Church. Easter. Matthew. The terms rolled around in her mind. "All right. I will," she said softly, surprising herself. He reached across the table and lightly touched her hand.

Strangely, she felt like a child again. Little and small and trusting. Longing to see the face of Jesus. What she saw, instead, were the beautiful burning eyes of Matthew Carr, staring into the depths of her very soul.

CHAPTER 4

"YOU'RE GOING WHERE?" Taylor asked in disbelief as he leaned against the curtained wall of Catlin's apartment.

"Church," she told him again. "Tomorrow is Easter Sunday, and I'm going to church with Matthew Carr."

"You can't be serious?" His expression hovered somewhere between condescending amusement and agitation.

"Good grief, Taylor! It *is* Easter Sunday. People *do* go to church."

He raked his hand through his hair and considered her as she sat curled up on her sofa. The remains of their candlelight dinner lay nearby on a round oak table. A fire blazed in the fireplace behind her, igniting the fiery strands of her hair in its glow.

"Look, I didn't mean for you to take this assignment so literally. You don't have to date the guy in order to check him out."

She jumped to her feet. "That's unfair, Taylor! It isn't a *date!* He simply asked me to go to church with him. I said yes. Then I'm going to a small party he's throwing for his campaign staff out at his estate."

Relief flooded his features and his blue eyes lost their edge of suspicion. "Oh," he said, "I see. You're just using the church bit to get to that party for an inside look at things. That's better. Why didn't you just say so in the first place?"

Her anger swelled again. No, that wasn't true. She was going to church with him because she wanted to. And she had no intention of using his invitation to dig around for a story. But one look at Taylor told her that he had drawn his own conclusions and that she wasn't going to dissuade him without an argument.

She sighed and flopped back down on the sofa. He crossed the room and sat next to her, draping his arm over her shoulders and drawing her close to him. He pressed his lips against her ear and nuzzled her neck. She wasn't in any mood for his caresses.

"What do you think about God?" she asked casually.

He jerked away to look at her incredulously. "*What?*"

"Don't you ever wonder about God?"

He snorted in disgust. "You have the strangest timing, woman. . . ."

She pushed farther away from him and scrutinized him coolly. "After hearing Matthew, I started thinking about my own relationship with God. Don't you ever think about yours?"

"Look," he fumed, "God never did me any favors. What I've gotten, I've gotten on my own. Hard work . . . lots of blood, sweat, and tears. Frankly, I had it a lot harder than Carr ever did. All he had to do was marry money. He never scraped for anything. So, of course, it's easy for him to be on good terms with God."

Taylor's cynicism surprised her. "Do you know Matthew Carr?"

Taylor hedged, studying her through narrowed eyes. "Why do you ask?"

"Well, if you've never met him and still hate him, it's not very fair. If you do know him and hate him, then *why?*"

He let out his breath in one long sigh. "I have never met him except on the most casual of terms. It's just my nature, Cat. I suspect anyone whose motives are chiseled on stone tablets of 'goodness' and 'pious integrity'."

"You'd rather he be out for himself?" she asked. "Like Cleaver? How does that mentality serve anyone?"

"I can't explain it," he snapped, standing swiftly and ending their discussion. "I just don't believe he's for real. I think there's more beneath the surface than anybody knows, and if you discover what it is, then Catlin Burke and WTSB will have the news scoop of the decade. Naturally, such an exposé will increase both our ratings and your credibility with viewers in this state."

He paused, his blue eyes bright with the intensity of his feelings. "Now, I think I'd better be going. . . ." He cut off her questions and crossed to the coat closet near the front door.

Confused, Catlin leaped up and followed him. She hadn't meant to drive him away. But there were so many unanswered questions. "You don't have to go. . . ." she said, watching him put on his coat.

He smiled wryly. "You've got church in the morning, remember?" He tossed off the words with a cutting edge in his voice. Suddenly he seized her by her shoulders and pulled her roughly to him, kissing her hard on the mouth. "Don't be duped . . ." he warned as he opened the door. She watched him leave, unable to comprehend either his attitude or his warning.

She wandered around for a few minutes, clearing

59

the table, her mind deep in thought. The buzz on her intercom caused her to gasp and jump, almost dropping a load of dishes. "Yes?" she asked into the box on the wall.

"It's Sam," crackled the familiar voice of the building's security guard. "There's a package for you down here, Miss Burke. You want me to send it up?"

"Yes, Sam. And thanks." Curiosity pricked at her. Who would be sending her something at this hour?

The package arrived shortly, wrapped in plain brown paper, thick and rectangular in shape. She sat on her hearth, in front of the dying embers of the fire and tore off the wrapper. It was a book. Moreover, it was a Bible, beautifully bound in thick ivory-colored leather. The pages were trimmed in gold and it smelled fresh and newly inked.

She flipped it open. On the inside cover, in bold black letters she read: "April 20/Easter To Catlin Burke. May God richly bless you. Hebrews 11:1. Matthew Carr"

She felt deeply touched by his gift. Curiously, she turned to the Book of Hebrews and read the verse he had meant for her to have. "Faith . . . the assurance of things hoped for . . . the evidence of things not seen. . . ." The words ran over and over in her head. Faith. Faith of the Puritans. Faith of the Christians involved in Matthew's campaign. Faith she wondered about for herself.

Thoughtfully she ran her fingers over the rippled grain of the Bible's surface as the dying fire turned to pale gray ashes.

Matthew's church was not at all like she expected it to be. It was a small, white clapboard building, with a single spire standing white and tall in the bright sunlight of the crisp, clean April morning. Tucked away in the quiet hills, it was filled to overflowing, but even so there were less than two hundred people squeezed into the old oaken pews.

There were no gigantic stained-glass windows. No stone or brick or brass. Only the simple rising of an altar in the front, a clear circular window mounted behind it, allowing sunlight to stream through in thick pools of buttery yellow.

The altar was adorned simply, with a single golden cross, gleaming and triumphant, surrounded by masses of glorious white lilies. An organist played victorious music of resurrection and Catlin sat still and tranquil next to Matthew in a pew near the front. She was a child again.

Memories washed over her, bringing back youthful longings. It had been so long since she had sat in the house of God. Too long. She stole a look at Matthew from the corner of her eye. He looked elegantly handsome in a dark navy worsted wool suit. A beam of sunlight from one of the long windows next to the aisle bounced off his thick brown hair and intensified the green in his eyes.

She smoothed her hand across the pale yellow skirt of her tailored linen suit and touched the cameo pinned at the throat of her gray silk blouse. People had stared at them when they had entered the church, some nodding at Matthew, some whispering and pointing at her. The pattern was familiar. After all, she *was* Catlin Burke. People recognized her all the time.

Now, sitting next to him, losing herself in the sanctity of the moment, it didn't matter who she was. Only that she was here, in a quaint and traditional little church, preparing her heart to receive the Word of God. She knew that Taylor would think it corny and trite.

The minister surprised her, too. He was a very young man—probably not more than thirty—not at all the image of ministers she held from her youth. But his voice was resonant, his message exhilarating and uplifting, his content centering on the miracle of the

61

Resurrection. As he spoke, she let his words melt over her, and she let go of her mind and absorbed the beauty of the moment. She had forgotten how peaceful it was in the presence of God; how beautiful and pure and lovely it could be in His house. . . .

She was glad she had come. Glad Matthew had asked her. Grateful that she felt, that somehow— even after all this time apart from Him—God remembered her.

"Enjoy the service?" Matthew asked Catlin ˌ ˑ.
They stood on the rolling lawn at the back of his great mansion. People—campaign workers, their families and children—spilled over the soft grass, still dressed in their Easter Sunday finery. Thankfully, the weather was warm and balmy.

"Yes, very much. I'm ashamed to tell you how long it's been since I've been to church. But I certainly felt right at home there this morning."

"You once told me you were raised in the church," he reminded her.

She felt like she owed him more information about herself. "My father was a postal worker. My mother, a nurse. I was their one and only. Their pride and joy. They made sure I had the best they could possibly give me. Church was part of that. Their interpretation of the 'American Dream'," she added with a wry smile. "Church attendance was expected of me—just like going to college." She fell silent, lost in poignant memories.

He watched her intently. She sensed it and blushed slightly. "My parents still live in that quiet little neighborhood in Ohio where I grew up. They feel very proud of my accomplishments. . . ."

"You don't?" he asked, his eyebrows arching over his beautiful eyes.

She grew flustered. What was the matter with her? Why was she pouring her heart out to a political candidate *she* was supposed to be investigating?

She shook off her melancholia and struggled to regain a less intimate dialogue. "Let's say, I lost some things along the way." Then she turned and gazed at the clusters of people surrounding the bricked patio and sloping lawn. "Now, who are all these people?" she asked brightly, changing the subject.

"Let me introduce you." He took her elbow and led her to the nearest group. The familiar faces of Neal and Dodd beamed at her through the round of introductions. Their wives, Lynda and May, offered her cheerful, unaffected smiles.

"Such golden eyes!" the slim red-haired May Brighton exclaimed. "Honestly, TV doesn't do you justice."

"Maybe it's your color control," Catlin quipped, self-conscious in the spotlight of their attention . . . The public was always curious; always eager to know more about her. She guarded her personal life zealously, allowing very few people a glimpse inside her private world. "Matthew tells me you and your husband will handle PR for his campaign."

"It's a big job," May conceded. "But even though I've been out of the business for several years, it's all coming back to me."

"Brilliantly, too, I might add," Neal touched his wife's cheek. "But Matthew's campaign is worth it. *Matthew* is worth it," he stated flatly.

"You know, Catlin," Matthew quietly interjected, "there's a gigantic morality gap between our country's leaders and its people. The people actually believe one thing. The politicians—the shakers and movers—believe quite another."

"I've gathered some interesting statistics," May added. "I'd be happy to share them with you." All at once twin, blond-haired boys about eight years old, erupted into their midst, each shouting at May about some injustice at the hands of the other.

"Slow down, boys!" she commanded. Then she

dropped to a crouch and listened intently to each one's story. "Is that really worth fighting over?" They drooped their blond heads. "What do you think Jesus would want you to do?"

The boys glanced at each other and one mumbled, "He'd want us to love one another."

"Is this the way you love? Each of you guys demanding your own rights? Isn't there a better way?"

They shook their heads, then looked shyly at each another and muttered sheepish "I'm sorry's." Within minutes, they had solved their differences and were bounding off toward a giant oak tree down near the winding brook at the foot of the lawn.

"Excuse me," May smiled, apologizing for the interruption.

But Catlin was fascinated. She had never before heard a mother relate to her children in quite that way. How different were these friends of Matthew!

Once again, her mind tracked other parties, other people. Station personnel parties. Parties where people talked shop, drank too much, and became overly loud and self-serving. In fact one such example, Taylor's annual summer employee party, was months away, but already she dreaded it.

Matthew took her elbow, and she dragged her mind back to the present. "Everybody wants to meet you," he reminded her, taking her from group to group, introducing her to his friends. Each group made her feel welcome and special. It nagged at her that Taylor distrusted Matthew so much. Ate at her that she was *really* supposed to be investigating Matthew. So far, he seemed above reproach.

Still, there was Sandra. Like a dark shadow, her presence clouded the joy in Catlin's day. "I think I need to powder my nose," she told Matthew just as waiters in white coats wheeled out carts laden with food. The pungent aroma of barbeque ribs vied with the flowery fragrance of spring.

64

"Don't be too long," he told her, squeezing her hand.

She made her way into the house, weaving through clusters of people chatting amiably and children playing hide and seek. The back wing of the mansion, the kitchen area, and sun porch bustled with activity. But as she walked deeper and deeper into the interior of the old house, quiet descended, enveloping her like a cloak.

Her heels moved silently over the exquisite carpets, and clicked smartly over the marbled foyer floor. She had a destination in mind and within minutes, she was standing at the foot of the enormous portrait on the blue-carpeted landing. The immobile woman on the canvas towered above Catlin, causing her to feel tiny, insignificant. Sandra stared down like ancient royalty, frozen in time, forever young, forever preserved from mortal decay.

She had lived. She had breathed. She had lain in Matthew's arms. Catlin allowed her imagination to envision the woman standing next to her husband. What great sadness lay behind her haunted eyes? What secret was forever locked in her past?

"I've been looking for you!" Matthew's voice from the foot of the stairs caused her to whirl. She flushed, embarrassed, like a small child caught with her hand in the cookie jar. "I–I'm coming . . ." she stammered. But she didn't move.

In three long strides, Matthew closed the distance between them. His eyes looked troubled and wary as he caught her hands and slowly pulled her toward him. She was drawn to him as if by some magnetic force. She knew she should retreat. It would take only a simple step backward; yet she could not bring herself to move.

And suddenly, she didn't want to move. She wanted to be in his arms, to feel the pressure of his lips against hers. It would have happened, too, if her eyes had not drifted over his head, to the portrait behind him. Sandra Carr rose above him, a specter in pale blue satin. A siren from another time . . . another life.

"Hey, Matthew!" Neal's voice, calling from the hallway, impinged on the moment. "Your public awaits!"

Catlin caught her breath and struggled to control the trembling of her hands and the hammering of her heart. "I'm coming!" Matthew called down to Neal. He turned and offered her his hand. "Won't you come with me?"

Catlin nodded mutely and fairly fled down the stairs of the landing—down the long hall and out into the clean, sweet April air, toward the sounds of laughter and gaiety and the company of flesh-and-blood people. She went as far and as fast as she could go, away from the cloying presence of the past—and the lifeless face of Sandra Carr.

"How was church?" Taylor didn't even try to disguise the contempt in his voice.

Catlin sat on the edge of the velour sofa in his office, sipping a cup of freshly brewed coffee. Outside, the Monday morning sunlight streamed into the garden of WTSB. Several robins bobbed and flitted in a tree bursting with the new green leaves of spring.

Catlin ignored his sarcasm and continued scanning the pages of her week-long agenda. "Fine." She had no intention of sharing with Taylor the beauty and emotion she had felt at the Easter service.

"The party?" he queried.

"That was fine, too." She flashed him a dazzling smile.

He glowered at her momentarily, then his voice took on a more professional tone. "Are you ready for the campaign trail?"

"Yes," she told him. *More than ready*, she thought

to herself. She was aching to get off in the country-side, to follow and report on Matthew's effect on the people around the state. She flipped open her file folder and handed Taylor a copy of her upcoming schedule.

"We'll go into the interior first, hitting Worcester and then Springfield. Next, we'll swing west and north, to include every town between here and Pittsfield; then back to Fitchburg, Lowell and then home to Boston. It's an eight-day tour. I expect it to be hectic and very busy." She added, "I understand that Matthew . . . uh . . . Carr has two more whistle stop tours planned. One in midsummer, along the coast from Gloucester and the Cape; then another in early fall, around New Bedford/Providence areas. Naturally, there will be several overnighters, but I expect him to concentrate most of his time and energy here in Boston and outlying areas, where most of the votes are garnered."

Taylor looked over the schedule and laid it on his desk. "He's also going to be at the big Charity Ball in June—to do his social 'thing,' no doubt, and make inroads with all those bluebloods that came with his wife's family ties," Taylor commented, not too kindly.

The Charity Ball. Catlin knew about it. She had reported on it for both the news show and her own talk show, 'Inside,' for the past three years. It was the kickoff of the summer social season, a benefit for several popular organizations, a hospital or two, and work by the Historical Society. Taylor always attended. In fact, everybody who was anybody attended the lavish affair.

"I'll be going this year, too," he said. "Plan to come with me."

She leaned forward. "What?" she asked, confused. "As a reporter?"

"As my date." A note of irritation crept into his

voice. "Good grief, Cat, I thought you knew by now that I care for you. I want you with me . . . especially in public."

She wasn't sure how to respond. It would be interesting to attend as a guest and not as a reporter for a change. But such an appearance would also further cement her growing personal relationship with Taylor. Was that what she wanted? Gathering up her papers, she mumbled her acceptance and headed back for her own office. She definitely needed some time alone to think.

Her head, her heart were in turmoil. Taylor cared about her. He loved her. But how did she feel about him? And did his increasing interest in her have anything to do with her involvement with Matthew? So many questions! So many conflicting emotions! She shook her head, trying to clear it.

Her mind wasn't on the staff meeting, but once it was over, she fairly growled at Maggie, "I want to see you in my office. And bring your file."

Maggie raised her eyebrows, tossed her head of frizzy hair and scurried off to do Catlin's bidding.

She entered the office in a huff a few minutes later. Catlin regretted the rude way she had spoken to the woman. Maggie could be both an asset and a liability. Either way, it wouldn't do to alienate her now.

"Yes?" the older woman asked testily.

"I'm sorry, Mag," she apologized. "It's been a zoo around here lately, and I have a lot on my mind."

Maggie shrugged and pulled a chair closer to the desk to accept the mug of steaming hot coffee Catlin was pouring for her. "Before I take off on the campaign trail, I need to have all you can possibly give me about Carr."

"His background isn't quite as glamorous as his wife's," Maggie confided as she flipped through the file in her hands. "Actually, he was quite middle-class until Sandra came along. Oh, he was a brilliant student. Grew up in Springfield. His father died ten years ago. His mother lives with a sister in Florida.

"But he was also an excellent athlete. Went through college on a football scholarship. He probably would have gone on to the pros, but then he met Sandra." Catlin closed her eyes and let Maggie's words infuse her memory cells. She pictured Matthew as he must have looked, in football pads and jersey. No wonder the little rich girl fell for him!

"Their wedding was an event . . . with a capital 'E'," Maggie said drolly. "Surprisingly he fit right in with her family. Old man Van Cleef favored Carr greatly . . . took him into the business and gave him his empire on a silver platter."

Maggie flipped over a few more pages and scanned them briefly. "Since Sandra's death, he's become very active in things Christian. Joined some little church up in the hills and severed most of his former ties with big business, the social register and longtime Van Cleef associates. But," she cautioned, "he's still a prominent and powerful man in this state. He wields a lot of power in the financial hierarchy."

Catlin felt a question rolling around in her brain. She didn't want to ask it. But she had to know the answer. "Other women?" She tried to keep her tone businesslike.

"A few dates. No one in particular."

Catlin wasn't sure if she were relieved or not. If there was no one special in his life, did it mean that he still grieved for his dead wife?

"Is that it?" Catlin asked crisply, trying to focus her thoughts on her discussion with Maggie.

"Yes and no."

"Meaning?"

"Rumors," Maggie stated. "Hard to pin down the specifics. The very rich guard their own like jealous attack dogs."

"For instance." Catlin grew wary. She trusted

Maggie's news savvy. The woman had a natural instinct for ferreting out information.

"Talk, mostly," Maggie suggested. "Bottom line, however, is that Carr and Sandra did not have a marriage made in heaven."

The words sounded ugly and distasteful. An unhappy marriage. Yet, he had seemed so protective of his dead wife. Or maybe it was himself he was protecting. . . . "Are you sure?"

"Let me do some more checking. Maybe I'll know more by the time you get back." Maggie stood and gulped the last of her coffee.

"I want you to dig, Maggie," Catlin said from the swivel chair behind her desk. "There's so much innuendo that doesn't jibe with the man I'm beginning to know."

Maggie nodded, hesitated, then said cautiously, "Taylor wants an exposé. I can see that. What do *you* want, Catlin?"

"The truth," she stated firmly. "Only the truth."

After Maggie left, Catlin sat staring into space. She couldn't reconcile the conflicting images of Matthew in her mind. On the one hand, there was Matthew gaining power, prestige, and social position through marriage, albeit an unhappy union between the wealthy society girl and the brilliant young man. On the other, there was Matthew, the self-proclaimed Christian. A man who hoped to carry the banner of God's truth into the machinery of social and civil justice. It was all very perplexing.

And there were also her own feelings for him. He intrigued her. He fascinated her. He was a puzzle she found alluring and tantalizing. She recalled the nearness of him the afternoon before on the steps of the landing. The recollection sent a surge of warmth through her. He was so totally *masculine*. He aroused emotions in her that no other man had ever stirred. Passionate emotions. But also, deep longings and yearnings she could not identify.

70

She looked forward to the campaign trail. Looked forward to being near him day and night. Puzzles were meant to be solved. She determined to get inside him. Resolved to delve into his innermost core. She was, after all, a reporter. Expertly trained. Carefully groomed. If Matthew Carr had clay feet, Catlin Burke would find them.

CHAPTER 5

CATLIN RESTED HER HEAD against the cushioned seatback of the bus and stared out of the window through the curtain of fine drizzling rain. She heard the slapping of tires on the road's surface and closed her eyes, lulled by the low buzz of conversation surrounding her.

The bus was only half full of newspaper, radio, and TV reporters, their crews and boxes of equipment. She knew that others would join them in cities along the way, but so far Matthew's campaign tour had gotten off to a very slow start.

True, a large number of Christian media people were on the tour, but few of the state's big stations and newspapers had sent along personnel. Most had assumed a "wait-and see" attitude. If Matthew did well in the polls, they would join his next tour. It was the classic contradiction of getting exposure in the press in order to get exposure in the press.

The networks hadn't sent any reporters or crews either. Most of the interest in the Massachusetts senatorial race still centered on Cleaver. His campaign entourage was large; his appearances, well-covered and heavily financed. *How does he get away with it?* Catlin wondered. His mishandling of his office was obvious and blatant, yet he was still politically strong and leading in the polls. It would be hard to unseat an incumbent, and Matthew clearly had a long, hard uphill battle.

Matthew himself sat in the front of the bus, speaking with two reporters from small Christian newspapers. Next to Catlin was Sue Davis, going over the material passed out to each crew by Dodd. Red McIvers, the cameraman, sat across the aisle, talking shop with a colleague from a rival Boston station.

She recognized only one other on-air personality on the bus—the newspaper reporter from the *Boston Globe*. Leo Kelly's reputation as a crack political reporter was legend. Tough as nails, terse, and direct, Leo had an incredible instinct for the political scene. He sat now, in his slightly rumpled brown suit and a sports shirt open at the neck, looking over the busload of people with his hard, cynical gaze. Interesting, thought Catlin, that he had chosen to accompany Matthew's campaign and not Senator Cleaver's. Leo Kelly was astute and respected. His opinion would count with hundreds of voters.

At that moment his gaze fell on her, and a look of contempt crossed his leathery face. She had seen that look before. A lot of newspaper people wore it when confronting television reporters. Dyed-in-the-wool newspaper journalists had little grace and regard for television 'newsies,' whom they considered light-weights in the world of serious journalism.

No matter, she told herself. She had been proving for years that she wasn't just a pretty piece of fluff and that she could make it in this man's world. She certainly didn't need Leo Kelly's approval. Deliberately avoiding his gaze, she concentrated on her intended upcoming coverage.

Matthew was to speak at a veterans' meeting in Worcester at noon. Then he had two tapings at small radio stations that afternoon in the city. She made several notes.

After a night in an area hotel, the bus would roll on to Springfield. They would spend three days there, where Matthew was already scheduled for three radio stations and a TV talk show, and had four speaking engagements. And on and on, from town to town, day after day, until they finally rolled back into Boston at the beginning of the next week.

Catlin's job was to send back daily taped reports concerning her observations of the excitement level of the campaign, Matthew's progress in meeting the people, and public reaction. She was determined to present him as fairly as possible, without the cynicism and derision that often crept into other news reporters' work when faced with such high ideals and unworldly standards. Matthew believed in his destiny, his calling. She would present it to the voters in a fresh, unbiased manner. Then *they* would decide his fate at the polls in November.

"How do you want to approach this?" Sue asked, causing Catlin to retreat from her deep thoughts.

"I like the angle of the 'American Dream'," Catlin said to the serious, plain-faced girl sitting next to her. Sue was fresh out of college, with a degree in mass communications. But she was good—sharp and technically competent to direct, edit, and run camera and sound.

They would have to send their tapes ready to go on the air. Therefore, they didn't have the luxury of spending hours editing and pasting together a story. Sue would make sure everything was technically correct. Catlin had creative control. She would write and perform the unfolding campaign story. Red would run the mini-cam, lug and carry the equipment boxes, and set up the taping shoot. By the end of the tour, they would be a solid unit, an integrated team. Newspaper men, like Leo Kelly, only needed a portable typewriter and a telephone to get his stories back. But he had much stricter deadlines.

"'The American Dream'?" Sue asked.

"The reasons Europeans migrated here," Catlin defined. "History tells us that many came to flee religious persecution. Matthew believes that God honored the faith of our founding fathers with His blessings. But somewhere along the way, issues got muddied, distorted." She groped for the right words. "Eventually freedom took on a different meaning. It became a panacea for living a life without rules and restrictions. The old 'do your own thing' philosophy. The attitude of 'if-it-feels-good, do it'."

Sue tapped her pencil against her open palm thoughtfully. "So we've redefined freedom and carried it to an unrealistic extreme?"

"Exactly!" Catlin nodded. "According to Matthew, we've become so free that we release criminals into society, expose ourselves to all sorts of pornography, and look out for personal interests at every turn."

"And that's what Carr's running against?"

"Yes," said Catlin. "He's not against freedom. He's against *undisciplined* freedom. A return to biblical standards gives society rules and standards. And ironically, a surprising amount of freedom. . . ."

Sue nodded, the light of revelation spreading over her face. "No wonder you want to cover his campaign," she said. "He could be a very important political influence over the next few years."

Guiltily Catlin agreed, knowing that she was also out to destroy him if she found any falseness or duplicity in his intentions. Taylor was right about one thing. A reporter could never lose objectivity. Once that happened, he or she would become a puppet and not a proclaimer of truth.

She watched Matthew intently. His charm, good looks and infectious smile had completely captivated the reporters seated near him. Catlin was not unimpressed. But she fought to remain detached. The success of her venture depended on it. Absently, she wrote the name *Sandra* across the top of her file folder. The very word was an antidote to the charisma of the handsome man seated in the front of the bus!

Catlin made sure Red got plenty of tape footage of Matthew mingling with the people during the hectic day following their arrival in Worcester. Lots of shots displaying his warm and open manner. Then she taped a stand-up piece in front of an American flag, summing up his veterans speech and radio interviews. She wrapped it up with more shots of people surging forward to shake Matthew Carr's hand, touch his clothing, feel his presence.

The impression he left was one of confidence and sincerity. He was a man who spoke with authority and who radiated belief in his dream. Once Catlin wrapped the story, Red had a taxi take the tape to the airport. It would arrive in Boston in time for the eleven o'clock news. She knew that Taylor would preview it first. She hoped he approved.

The various crews congregated in a small diner near the hotel Neal and Dodd had chosen as the base of operations for the media. One room in the small hotel contained tables and several typewriters. Leo Kelly sat, pounding at the keys until late in the evening. Catlin longed to know what he was writing, itched to know his opinion of Matthew. But, like the rest of the state, she would have to read it in the paper.

She crawled between the sheets that night, bone-weary, and with the realization that she hadn't spent a minute alone with Matthew. She felt strangely deflated at the thought. The campaign trail wasn't going to give her much time with him at all. There was just too much for him to do. Too many others demanding his time.

Catlin punched her pillow and buried her face in it. She missed him. . . . Already she missed his undivided attention. . . .

"What you're telling me then, Mr. Carr, is that a return to Christian standards will solve all our country's problems?" The dark-haired talk show host leaned in toward Matthew on the set of his morning show. Though he smiled congenially, there was subtle sarcasm and ridicule in his voice.

Unperturbed, Matthew grinned into the interviewer's smug expression and answered, "Yes, Mr. Shelby. That's exactly what I'm saying. You see," he continued, "as a nation we do have standards. Morality is continually being legislated. The question is: Whose morality? Do we live by the standards of situational ethics—if it's right for this moment in time, let's do it—or do we live by the standards laid down by God and set forth by those who framed this nation's constitution?"

Catlin sat in the Springfield television studio, watching the familiar activity around her. So often she had hosted the interview shows. Today, she was merely a member of the audience, like the rest of the reporters who had chosen to attend the taping of Matthew's latest interview.

From the corner of her eye, she watched Leo Kelly's pen scratching furiously on his notepad. His face was an inscrutable mask, yet he was drinking in every word Matthew uttered. *What are you thinking, Mr. Kelly?* she mused to herself. *Do you see Matthew as a man of vision or an advocate of noble, but impractical ideals?* In the long run, men like Leo Kelly would make or break Matthew's bid for office. Matthew Carr might persuade Christians to vote for him, but he also had to persuade a lot of non-

Christians—people who were just plain fed up with corruption, double standards, and a lack of serious political leadership.

Mr. Shelby glanced at his floorman and received the hand cue to wrap it up. "One more question before we close," Shelby said. "Many of our viewers consider themselves upright and moral. Yet, you've said they lack standards. How can this be?"

Catlin's blood raced. That wasn't at all what Matthew said! Shelby was contending that Matthew was an intellectual snob, looking down on the common man.

"In God, there is no class or race or sexism," Matthew said sincerely. "We are truly equal. Many of us live by standards in our personal lives, but we fail to carry them over into our businesses, our politics. As a senator, I expect to hold fellow legislators accountable for their actions. I expect to back legislation that aligns with the standards of both the Bible and the Constitution. Our forefathers believed in the dream of 'one nation, under God.' Frankly, so does Matthew Carr."

Once the camera light flicked off, Shelby shook Matthew's hand, the audience stood to leave and the studio crew began the process of breaking down the set. Catlin side-stepped the busy station personnel and walked over to Matthew.

"Hello!" He smiled warmly at her. As usual, her pulse quickened. "How'd it go?" She knew he was asking for her professional opinion.

"You did well," Catlin affirmed. "But Shelby is a fool. He kept trying to trip you up instead of probing for facts to inform his viewers."

Matthew laughed. "I'm used to it. If you're going to take a stand as a politician, then you'd better be prepared for a lot of pot shots."

As he spoke, Catlin noticed tiny lines of weariness etched around his eyes. It tugged at her heart to know

78

how tiring and draining his campaign must be. She wanted to reach out and touch him, but she knew she didn't dare. She had no right.

"Sorry, Matthew," Neal announced, crossing the studio with long strides, "but you've got a radio show to do in an hour. We'd better roll."

Matthew nodded and pressed his thumb against his temple. "Of course," he told Neal. "Let's go. . . ." He turned to Catlin and said, "I haven't seen nearly enough of you on this tour. I'm sorry. Maybe when we get back to Boston. . . ." His words filled her with anticipation.

She dropped her eyes and gave a noncommittal nod, but her heart responded with a lurch. She watched him hurry out of the studio. Abruptly she turned to gather her belongings and found herself looking straight into the lively, inquisitive eyes of Leo Kelly. She flushed and shoved her notes into her briefcase, planning to catch a cab back to the hotel, prepare a script, then round up Sue and Red for their daily tape session.

"Share a cab?" Leo Kelly invited.

Surprised that the surly journalist had acknowledged her presence, Catlin agreed hesitantly.

The cab arrived and they rode together in wary silence. She respected the man. He was, after all, one of the top journalists in the country. But he was also downright unfriendly, having pointedly snubbed everyone on the press bus.

"Want some lunch?" the older, heavyset man invited.

Catlin, taken aback, agreed, still confused by his sudden attention.

He took her to a deli near the hotel, heavy with the aroma of corned beef and dill pickles. "You want a beer?" he asked. She shook her head. "That's the trouble traveling with a bunch of Christians," Kelly muttered under his breath. "Not a decent elbow-bender in the lot."

His gruff manner began to amuse her. She would probably like him if she let herself. They ordered sandwiches and sat in one of the booths, upholstered in bleak, brown vinyl. After a few bites eaten in silence, Leo Kelly looked over at her. "So, what do *you* think his chances are?"

Why would Leo Kelly want her opinion about the election? He had been openly contemptuous of her throughout the trip.

"I think that if people *really* listen to what he's saying, he'll be elected," she told him. "What do you think?"

Kelly countered with another question. "Would you vote for him?"

"Yes."

"Why?" he asked, his hard eyes staring at her from folds of leathery flesh.

"Cleaver is powerful and has important connections. But there are serious questions concerning his integrity. Nolan lacks color and personality. Besides, he's a one-issue candidate. He can't do the job."

Leo nodded in agreement. "You're absolutely right. In two months, I predict that Nolan will be out of the race. But Cleaver might manage to keep the lid on his investigators until after the election. Carr's got to get a broad base of support if he's going to pull this one off."

"Are you going to help him?" she asked the older reporter pointedly.

"Don't know yet." Leo flipped a wadded napkin onto the formica tabletop. He asked, "You a Christian?"

She felt caught off balance by his question. Was she? The memories of Easter Sunday came to her. The feelings of contentment and peace. The sense of wonder she had experienced in Matthew's church. "I—I was once . . ." she hedged. "Matthew Carr's campaign has caused me to do some thinking . . ."

80

She glanced over at him, expecting to see ridicule and derision on his face. She saw neither.

"I'm not," Kelly volunteered, "but Matthew Carr is going to need people like us. Any political system that depends on the average man for its perpetuation, like ours does, needs all the help it can get."

"You're a very cynical man, Mr. Kelly," she observed.

"I've been around for a long time," he reminded her. "Political talk is cheap. But I do like all this business about old-fashioned ideals and principles and the American Dream that Carr espouses. Maybe I'm a fool, but Matthew Carr does feel like a breath of fresh air."

"Why do you care what I think?"

He almost smiled at her. "I watch you sometimes on the tube. I used to think that any woman who looked like you couldn't have anything else going for her." She bristled, but controlled her rising temper. "Now, after seeing how you've covered Carr this trip, I know there's something between your eyebrows and your hairline."

"Is that a compliment?" she asked incredulously.

"Miss Burke," the reporter said, "I assure you, it's not an insult."

Catlin watched Leo with an unflinching gaze. Would he personally back Matthew? Would he use his clout and influence to stand with Matthew's campaign issues? He wasn't a Christian. Yet, he seemed attracted and drawn to Matthew's political ideals.

"Do you know anything else about him? You've been in Boston a lot longer than I have. . . ."

His eyes narrowed as he chose his words carefully. "I knew the Van Cleefs. I knew Sandra. I knew she and Carr weren't happy."

Catlin's adrenalin pumped. "Sandra . . . what was she like?"

Leo Kelly regarded Catlin for a long hard moment

81

as if weighing his response on some inner scale. "She loved him," Leo said slowly. "With an obsession . . . a mania. He didn't love her back. And it cost her her life."

The press bus rolled out of Springfield, the Army rifle capital of the country, westward through gently rolling hills and terraces of green grass, into the ancient timeworn beauty of the Berkshire Hills. In a few hours, they arrived in Pittsfield, a town nestled in the shadow of Mount Greylock.

Catlin found the air and scenery invigorating, resplendent with patches of wildflowers, honeysuckle and climbing roses. Gracious elm-shaded streets, quiet residential areas, and a sedate business center graced the city itself. Expansive views of wide meadows, tree-lined streams and small lakes could be seen from the high plateau of the once famous resort city.

Catlin and Sue settled into their motel room after Matthew had delivered a speech at a local church. She made notes about the day's taping and sent Red off to scout for scenic places for the actual shoot. She had shared little time with Leo since the day before, but he had nodded at her while boarding the bus and she felt a bit more comfortable around him.

Putting in a call to Taylor, Catlin felt elation at the sound of his voice on the line. She *did* miss him.

"Hello, beautiful!" he said. "How's it going?"

"Tiring. But the scenery here is lovely."

"Well, babe, your reports are terrific!" She was warmed by his praise. She wanted him to like her work. "And," he continued, "eight days is too long for you to be away. I miss you."

She remembered the warmth of his arms and the tenderness of his kisses. She missed the familiarity of him. "Just a few more days," she promised.

"You take care of yourself," he said. "And get back to me as soon as you can," he added tenderly.

She recradled the phone and closed her eyes, trying to see his face in her mind's eye. She did, but with stubborn persistence, Matthew's face also floated into the chamber of her memory. She shook her head and chastised herself. Why did he fascinate her so? What was it about him that tantalized her senses, teased her soul, and stole her objectivity? It was Taylor she should be dreaming about. Not Matthew.

The next four days passed in a whirlwind of appearances, speeches, interviews, tapings and media coverage. The campaign bus traveled from city to city, town to town, community to community . . . south, then east through the state, back toward Boston.

Wherever he went, Matthew Carr caused people to stop and listen. None seemed put off by his avidly Christian stand, his call to return to the ideals and dreams of an earlier, simpler America. Catlin observed his appearances with the analytical mind of a seasoned reporter. These people were the descendants of those first hardy Americans. These were the average people, the common people. And they loved Matthew Carr. They understood his message. They believed in him.

The last night of the tour, following a dinner meeting and speech, Catlin left Sue reviewing the day's tape and wearily returned to their room to prepare for bed. Tomorrow she would be home. She longed for the familiar surroundings of her apartment: her furniture, her kitchen, her own bed. She had just turned out the light when a soft knock sounded against her door.

Sue must have forgotten her key, she thought. She opened the door a crack, leaving the chain in place.

"It's me," came Matthew's deep voice. She gasped with surprise. "I was just wondering," he whispered conspiratorially, "how'd you like to play hooky?"

"Hooky?"

"There's a county fair about twenty miles from here. I've rented a car. How about sneaking off with me to ride the ferris wheel?"

The thought of the adventure pushed away the cobwebs in Catlin's tired brain and, charged with adrenalin, she changed into jeans and a cotton blouse. Knotting the sleeves of a sweater around her neck, she slipped out the back door and in a very few minutes, they were speeding through the darkening evening. She giggled, delighted at the incongruity of the dignified senatorial candidate and the TV journalist escaping like a pair of college kids. He grinned back.

"What would the voters think to see the would-be Senator slipping off to the fair?" she teased.

"They'd wish they could have come along, too," he said and reached over and squeezed her hand. "I'm glad you did. . . ."

The brightly lit fairgrounds on the outskirts of town were beckoning as they pulled up in the parking lot that was nothing more than an old hayfield. She could smell the pungent aroma as they crushed the stalks beneath their feet. Placing her hand willingly in Matthew's, Catlin followed his lead toward the colored lights and calliope music. Her nose, too, had picked up an unforgettable whiff of hotdogs, popcorn, and cotton candy. Her eyes danced as they walked down the garish midway. Banks of game booths lined the narrow pathway, crammed with people and noise.

"How'd you like a stuffed animal?" Matthew asked after surveying the various games of skill.

"I'd like that one," she said, pointing at a large stuffed tiger with a silly smirk on its fuzzy face.

"It's yours!" Matthew snapped his fingers and picked up a rifle, positioning it against his shoulder. He took careful aim and fired. The moving duck at the front of the booth never flinched.

Catlin giggled. "You missed, sharpshooter!"

"Pulls to the left," he said, narrowing his eyes at the target. He aimed and pulled the trigger again. This time the duck dropped. After five more perfect shots, the attendant handed over the stuffed toy.

Catlin hugged it to her, a look of childish happiness illuminating her face. And when Matthew's hand again enveloped hers, she warmed at the firm pressure.

They looked into a tent and found a display of American handicraft and artwork. Catlin marveled at the collection of needlepoint and pottery. She was immediately attracted to an array of quilts, carefully stitched by farmers' wives. She imagined the many hard-working hands that had lovingly worked the intricate designs.

"Oh, Matthew," she whispered, spotting one particularly beautiful spread. "This one is magnificent!" Two large, golden rings lay entwined in the center, with trees, flowers, birds, and puffy clouds surrounding the rings, and a gold cross positioned above.

"It's a weddin' quilt," an elderly woman said from behind a makeshift table. "It's a pattern handed down from my great-great-grandma. . . . Purty ain't it?" The woman's clear blue eyes sparkled.

"It's gorgeous!" Catlin confirmed with renewed awe. "Did you make it?"

"Me and my church circle," the woman smiled, lighting up her blue eyes.

"Do you want it?" Matthew asked.

Catlin gasped and searched for words to refuse his generous offer.

"It's a marryin' quilt," the woman emphasized. "It's for a weddin' bed. You two gettin' married?"

Catlin flushed, feeling her cheeks grow hot. Matthew seemed amused. "I'll take it," he told the woman. He paid her, watched as she lovingly wrapped it in brown paper, then took the package and the tiger back to the car. He rejoined a still speechless Catlin outside the display tent.

"You shouldn't have. . . ."

"But I did," he told her, looking deeply into her golden eyes.

"Thank you. I'll always treasure it. How—how about a ride on the merry-go-round?" she asked brightly, attempting to cover the awkwardness she felt.

They crossed quickly to the red-topped carrousel and chose their painted, wooden steeds. "You'd better get a white one!" Catlin shouted as she swung up on a lacquered black pony.

He laughed at her and straddled a dazzling white horse with flared nostrils and flying mane. The calliope in the center of the carrousel started and slowly, slowly the overgrown toy began to turn. The wooden horses rose and fell in perfect rhythm. Catlin tossed her hair, clutched at the pole rising from the neck of her horse and watched as the world turned faster and faster, blurring the colors and the lights of the midway as she whirled past.

The only other person in her world was Matthew, rising and falling with the horse beneath him. Matthew . . . his eyes dancing, his smile joyous. Matthew . . . his muscled arms holding the makeshift reins. Matthew . . . his face . . . his mouth . . . his eyes.

Breathless and laughing, they jumped down as the carrousel slowed to a stop, its music wheezing to a halt.

"Come on!" he cried, grabbing her hand and pulling her toward the ferris wheel. She ran behind him and they scooted into the metal seat at the bottom just before the attendant started the machine.

Their basket seat rose higher and higher, taking them up into the soft dark night, above the lights and the music and the crowds. They grew quiet together, watching the earth fall away and the glittering lights of the fair sparkle and dance below. Catlin took a deep breath as silence engulfed them.

They rode around in one vast circle, seeing the ground rise and recede, hearing the noise grow loud and soft. Then, while they sat at the very top of the great wheel, the machine groaned, squeaked, and came to a swaying halt.

"What's wrong?" she asked looking over the side of the basket at the activity below. Men scurried around on the ground below, waving and sending arm signals to the curious passengers stranded on the ride.

"Maybe we broke it," Matthew joked.

Suddenly, Catlin felt vulnerable in the open seat.

"Don't worry," he said, slipping his arm around her shoulders and tugging her against him. "They'll get it fixed soon. Meanwhile," he urged, "lean back and enjoy. No crowds, no interviews, no schedules to keep."

She turned slightly and looked at him. The moon hung in the starlit sky behind him, leaving his handsome face shrouded in dark shadows. But she didn't need the moon to see him. She knew every inch of his face. And she grew acutely aware of his body next to hers. How snugly she fit against his side. He stroked the thickness of her hair, tangling his fingers in its fragrant masses.

Her heart danced like water over smooth stones. The soft breeze, the heady scent of night-blooming flowers filled her senses. They were alone—truly alone. Completely cut off from the pressures and confinements of the world below. Free beings, floating above the earth and the troubles and demands of their everyday lives.

He tipped her chin upward, with the knuckle of his forefinger. She felt his eyes scanning her face, felt the soft light of the moon hovering on the surface of her skin. He dipped his mouth to hers and she felt the warm and eager pressure of his lips against her own.

He did not release her. His kiss held her captive, his arms encircled her in a prison of protectiveness.

She felt like velvet, soft, pliable as the touch of his mouth awoke her sleeping senses. A deep, luscious warmth spread through her and she returned his kiss with abandon. It was as if the stars had taken aim at her mind and pulled her into their glittering midst.

The sudden lurch of the ferris wheel caused them to break contact, and they stared breathlessly at each another. Catlin gasped, amazed. Never had she felt like that in a man's arms. Never had a kiss so enraptured her. She almost reached to touch his face, as if to recapture the magic.

But Matthew withdrew. He slouched darkly in the corner of the descending basket, his hands curled into fists, his jaw clamped, tense and hard. The artificial lights of the midway lit his features and Catlin shivered, struck by his look of thunder. Confusion and frustration coursed through her, leaving her battered emotions in ruins.

"I shouldn't have," he said stiffly. "Forgive me. I'm sorry."

She stammered something in return. "It's all right . . . really. . . ."

"It's been so long," he said hoarsely. "I haven't wanted a woman . . . in so long. . . ." He stopped his confession abruptly.

Since Sandra . . . she finished for him in her mind. Sandra. The very word left a bitter taste in her mouth. A sad and bitter taste. Who was this woman who could reach beyond the grave and touch him? Who could command his loyalty even in the arms of another woman? Who could reach back through the years and beckon jealously to his heart?

CHAPTER 6

CATLIN VERY CAREFULLY AVOIDED MATTHEW during the duration of the campaign tour. It wasn't hard to do. His time was absorbed completely by the rigors of his campaign. She avoided his eyes whenever they did meet in crowded rooms or on the bus. She locked away the feelings and the memories of their night together. *I will not remember*, she told herself. *I will not think of him and what he made me feel.* She forced herself to concentrate on Taylor and the warm welcome he would give her when she arrived home.

She went to the station first. Her office was filled with roses. Every card read: "I missed you! Taylor."

When she tapped on his office door, Taylor crossed to open it, caught her in his arms and swung her off the floor, kissing her hungrily.

She gave him back kiss for kiss, clung to him in desperation, and forced herself to consider his love for her. But like a record with a worn and impish groove, her thoughts refused to budge. She saw Matthew's face, felt Matthew's arms, tasted Matthew's lips. For Catlin, it was a cruel and ironic homecoming.

In the solitude of her apartment, Catlin unpacked and rearranged her belongings. She had left the stuffed tiger in a motel room. She ran her hands over the package containing the quilt; she decided against opening it, but couldn't bear to part with it either. In the end she shoved it atop her closet shelf, still in its brown paper wrapping.

Her life did return to normal—slowly. She busied herself with her duties at the station. She persuaded Taylor to let her do some comparative reports on the other candidates. She worked feverishly. When she absolutely *had* to contact Matthew, she went through Neal or Dodd. She surrounded herself with a protective wall of people—anything to avoid being alone with him again.

In June, new polls showed that Matthew Carr had made substantial gains with the voters and was actually leading in several areas. Nolan was losing ground quickly. But Harold Cleaver was still the favorite and frontrunner. Catlin read Leo Kelly's column with great interest. He endorsed no one, but his insights were both astute and thought provoking.

At the beginning of July, Matthew would make another swing through the state. This time he would concentrate on the coastal areas. Catlin wanted to go, yet she was terrified of going. She had a job to do and she couldn't let her feelings get in the way. By now, Matthew had attracted national attention. Wherever he went, he was news. His speeches, interviews and debates with Cleaver and Nolan were well covered by AP, UPI, and the networks. Catlin knew that the next tour would be entirely different. Matthew Carr belonged to the public now.

June slipped into Massachusetts like a pretty girl in a summer dress. And with her, came the widely heralded Charity Ball—the big extravaganza before the beautiful people exited the city to their homes on the Cape, Hyannis, Martha's Vineyard.

Catlin dressed carefully for the event. As Taylor Shentell's date she would receive close scrutiny by the gossip columnists. It amused her to think that she was going to be news, too. Taylor, distinguished in a black tux, arrived at her front door in a limousine. His hair shimmered silver in the soft light. The appraising look on his face disclosed that she had chosen the right dress for the occasion.

She had chosen it purposefully. This night she wanted to be beautiful. The dress was the color of ripened peaches, floor-length, a float of fine silk overlaid with delicate lace. The lacy areas covered her shoulders and neck and then melted away in the back to expose the silky expanse of her honey-colored skin. She had had her hairdresser pile her thick auburn hair on top of her head. The effect was one of breathless elegance. Tonight, she had to admit, Catlin Burke was at her best.

The Ball was held at the Boston Regency, a fine, old hotel in the heart of the city. It had been built at the turn of the century and visited by kings, presidents and dignitaries up through the thirties. Then, it had fallen into disfavor with the elite, spiraling into a tailspin of decay and disuse. In the sixties, civic-minded groups had fought to return it to its former grand estate. They succeeded. Now, its stone façade and red-canopied entranceway had become a symbol of a bygone era and historic relevance. It was also capable of holding a crowd the size of the one attending this evening.

Catlin entered the Grand Ballroom on Taylor's arm. The vast room, already filled with lavishly dressed women and their escorts, was jewel-bright, glittering under a magnificent chandelier hung from the center of the elevated ceiling. Red satin panels lined the walls, and lush red carpets, swirled with patterns of black, covered the enormous floor. A small string orchestra dressed in black tails, was positioned in front of a dance area of oak parquet. Dinner tables, set with china, silver, and linen cloths, filled the remaining space in the room.

Taylor led her through the maze of tables, nodding to those who greeted them. "You're the most beautiful woman in the room," he whispered in her ear.

She arched an elegant brow and adroitly diverted his personal remark. "If they were to hold a jewelry sale right now, they could cure cancer."

He laughed and escorted her to their table. She sat and scanned the program while he spoke to several friends, admitting inwardly that she was looking forward to the evening and the opportunity to observe Boston's elite. Wherever she looked, old Boston wealth surrounded her. Obviously, the bluest bloods in town were out in force for the gala.

The Van Cleefs would have come . . . she thought absently, then rebuked herself for thinking it. But, as she sat and looked at the bejeweled and silk-draped women, she couldn't help remembering the portrait of Sandra in her elegant blue gown.

In her mind's eye, Catlin envisioned her as she would have looked . . . floating and drifting between groups . . . chatting about her summer activities on the Cape . . . smiling and nodding . . . accepting invitations to parties and luncheons—the perfect candidate's wife.

"What are you thinking about so hard?" Taylor's question caused her to jump and blush.

"It–it feels different being here as a guest and not as a reporter," she stammered.

He took her hand and gazed into her eyes. "If I have my way about it, from now on, you'll be coming as a guest every year. . . ."

Now what does that mean? she wondered.

An articulate master of ceremonies welcomed the crowd, announced the serving of the meal, and promised an evening of entertainment, prizes, and the finest orchestra in town. The meal arrived, served by waiters in tuxedos. For such a large gathering, Catlin considered the food superb.

They dined on salmon mousse, steak Diane, potatoes au gratin and fresh asparagus tips, followed by a delicious confection of flaky pastry layered with honey and walnuts. The tide of conversation ebbed and flowed, and the string orchestra provided a muted backdrop, punctuated by occasional trills of laughter.

Even here, among the rich and famous, Catlin felt curious glances as she and Taylor enjoyed the meal. Recognition. It came with the territory. And Taylor Shentell did not show up in public with just anybody. She knew that come morning, they would be mentioned in someone's social column. She hated that part of her lifestyle, but it was inevitable.

At a nearby table, Leo Kelly lifted his water goblet in a silent toast. She nodded, smiled, and he rolled his eyes in a look of bored disdain. She got his message and slyly crossed her eyes for his benefit. He guffawed loudly, causing heads to turn.

"Let's mingle," Taylor said, taking her hand and pulling her up beside him.

"Oh, Taylor . . ." she hedged, "why not just sit and soak it up?"

"No way. I want to show you off." He laid his hand possessively on the nape of her neck and Catlin stiffened. She didn't want to be "shown off" like one of Taylor's acquisitions, and she resented his inference. But she allowed him to lead her through the network of tables where he made random stops to speak, to laugh and introduce her to his friends.

She recognized many officials and dignitaries from throughout the city. She nodded and smiled at bank presidents, judges, boardroom chairmen and even forced herself to be polite to a particular official she had exposed in a corruption scandal two years before. At the edge of the parquet dance floor Taylor paused with her to listen to the music of the string orchestra. "Are you enjoying yourself?"

"Of course," she told him lightly, still ill-at-ease.

"You deserve this kind of life. You deserve to be a part of this."

"Oh, I don't know." She flipped her hand in a gesture of dismissal. "I like the life I have. At least I feel like I'm doing something worthwhile. I don't think I'm cut out for charity parties and social teas. . . ."

"I think you are," Taylor countered. His cryptic message was again lost on her. Yet before she could answer, a shadow fell across them where they stood. Catlin turned and looked up at the tall, broad-shouldered physique of Matthew Carr. Her heart lurched and her mouth went dry.

"Good evening, Miss Burke," he said in his deep quiet voice. "Taylor," he added as an afterthought. Beside her, Taylor grew rigid. Instantly her reporter's instincts reared.

Taylor acknowledged Matthew curtly. Catlin observed them, her every muscle taut, her every sense alert. Did she detect a certain reserve, a forced civility, a cool aloofness . . . something? As quickly as she perceived it, it vanished. Suddenly she couldn't be sure the elusive barrier had ever existed.

"May I dance with Catlin?" Matthew asked, his voice polite, his tone friendly.

Taylor glanced at her. "Better ask the lady. Cat?"

No! Yes! "That will be fine, Taylor," she said stiffly.

"I'll bring her back to your table."

"We're on the left—" Taylor began.

"I know where you are," Matthew cut in.

Taylor's eyes had grown hard and cold, like blue ice. He squeezed her hand, turned sharply and walked briskly through the maze of tables. Matthew reached out and took her hand in his. Catlin dropped her gaze, suddenly shy, almost afraid to be in his arms again.

94

"I won't bite," he chided and she allowed herself to look at him again. His green-flecked eyes peered into hers like beams of light in a darkened room. "Come," he said taking her into his strong arms. She willed herself to stop shaking, to say something witty and nonchalant. Yet it was as if her brain had turned to mush.

"You're lovely," he said in her ear.

"Didn't you bring someone?" she asked casually, straining to keep herself distanced from him.

"I came alone. If I showed up at one of these things with a date, the gossip columnists would have a field day. And then all the attention would be on my alleged love interest and not on my campaign."

She thought, *But you have been here before with a woman, haven't you, Matthew? And I'll bet the columnists talked then, too. When you came with your wife—Sandra.*

"Besides, the only woman I'd want to bring came with someone else." His statement was simple, but his meaning was unmistakable.

"Taylor has been very good to me . . ." she said defensively. "He gave me this marketplace on a silver platter."

"Is your career that important? Don't you ever think about tomorrow?"

Tomorrow? She had never thought about it like that. Her career was just something she did every day. It was all she had, really. "No, I guess not," she admitted. "I figure I have enough to handle just keeping up with today."

He said nothing, but she sensed his disapproval. And worse, she knew that what she had just told Matthew was a lie. Ever since he came into her life, she had felt yearnings and longings she didn't understand. And ever since the night on the ferris wheel, she had felt more lost, more hungry, more confused than ever.

95

The pressure of his hand against her back caused her muscles to tighten, her nerves to feel raw and exposed. Suddenly the room seemed to press in around her. She felt like Cinderella, too long at the Ball. Catlin wanted the music to stop, willing herself to remain indifferent and withdrawn from the man who held her so lightly in his arms.

Taylor. She wanted to return to the safety and comfort of the familiar. He didn't jumble her emotions and turn her insides to jelly. She felt secure with Taylor. He loved her. She didn't have to struggle with all these crazy mixed-up feelings when she was with him.

"Will you be coming on my next tour?"

"Of course. I'm a reporter. I'm assigned to your campaign and I'll be there until election day." *There!* she thought. That would certainly let him know his place in her life. He was a job to her. Just a job.

"Catlin," he said quietly. "Don't shut me out."

His plea knifed through her heart. *Shut him out?* But how could she let him in? How could she, when a part of his life was closed to her?

"I–I think I'd like to return to my table now." Her voice was low, hesitant. She avoided his eyes.

He bowed slightly, graciously, and led her back across the room. It seemed as if every head in the room turned to watch their progress. Taylor stood and took her arm possessively when they arrived at the table, his manner cool and strangely distant.

They sat together in silence for a few miserable moments. *Taylor,* she thought. *Touch me! Hold me!* But he didn't. He only sat and stared blackly at the receding figure of Matthew Carr.

"Have you read this?" It was the first thing Taylor said to her the next morning after she had answered the summons to his office. He slammed a folded newspaper down hard against his desk, rose, and began to pace angrily across the carpet.

"What is it?" Catlin asked, surprised to see him in such a state of agitation.

"Natalie Hartford's column," he spat vehemently. "I swear that woman should be muzzled!"

Catlin went to the desk and picked up the newspaper. The smiling picture of Boston's most noted social gossip columnist stared out at her. She scanned the article quickly.

Dateline: Boston's Charity Ball. All the beautiful people turned out like stars in the summer sky for THE official start of the summer season. Pretty, pretty, pretty . . . was this reporter's view. How chic, how elegant, how fanta- bulous! I came . . . I saw . . . I report. What was the stunning Catlin Burke doing in the arms of political superstar, Matthew Carr? Wasn't that Taylor Shentell sitting on the sidelines while his star anchorwoman and Mr. Carr waltzed to the tune of "I only Have Eyes for You"? . . .

Catlin felt her own ire rise, but decided against an outburst. Taylor was already angry enough. She plopped down the paper and shrugged. "Ignore it. It's just a bunch of prattle from an empty-headed woman."

He continued to fume. "I think snake-handlers would cringe to be alone with her. . . ."

Catlin touched his arm and stopped his restless pacing. "Taylor," she said more softly, "please, don't let her get to you. It's not worth the aggravation."

"I can't help it. You're mine, Cat. I don't like that woman's implication."

She bit off her response, but his possessiveness disturbed her. How typical of him! He didn't ask. He just assumed.

He wadded up the newspaper and hurled it into the trash can. "How are you coming on the Carr story?" he asked pointedly.

"What do you mean?"

"Well, you've certainly had plenty of time to dig up *something* on him. How about it?"

She felt disturbed and put off by his attitude. "So far, nothing," she said curtly.

"I find that hard to believe. I thought you said there might be something about his dead wife. . . ." He let the sentence hang like an accusation.

"Innuendo," Catlin snapped. "Rumors and innuendo. The same kind of stuff that made you so mad when Natalie Hartford used it. I have heard Sandra loved him deeply. I have heard that their marriage was not particularly happy. I know she died in a car crash. And I know he got every cent of the Van Cleef money when she died. That's all I know, Taylor. Certainly not enough to speculate about on camera," she finished, her voice sharp, her hands clenched.

Taylor eyed her coolly. "Are you telling me you're finished digging?"

"No, but I can't do my job if you're always pressuring me to find dirt where there may not be any. Now, if you'll excuse me . . . I have work to do. I still have a news program to get on the air!"

He did not respond. Finally she turned on her heel and stalked out of his office, down the cool, quiet corridors of the WTSB executive suite and into the icy cold studio to the six o'clock news set. She stood for a minute, trying to regain her composure.

Why was she so angry? Why had she attacked Taylor, her employer, her friend? What was the matter with her? Matthew Carr . . . Matthew Carr. . . . How had she allowed him to get inside her life so thoroughly?

The second campaign tour was entirely different from the first. The bus was crowded with media people, but this time most were from out of state—networks, independent cable news services, AP and UPI, plus a smattering of national magazine reporters.

Matthew Carr had become big news. Now the press followed him like a hound on a fox's trail. With dismay, Catlin observed the general chaos as she boarded the bus, and almost turned and got off.

"Miss Burke!" Leo Kelly called to her from an aisle seat toward the rear.

She waved and joined him, squirming down the aisle littered with boxes, luggage, and bags. "Thanks!" She edged into the seat next to him. "What a zoo!" She hoped Red and Sue could find seats for themselves.

"Disgusting, ain't it?" Leo asked, almost forcing a smile on his face. "I told you it would be different if Carr caught on with the public."

She recognized reporters and on-air personalities from the three major networks. For the most part, they appeared bored and hapless, reading books and papers, insulating themselves against the clamor surrounding them.

"I guess we locals don't count for much now," she commented with resignation.

Leo shrugged. "It happens. Let a guy like Carr get visible and members of the press descend like vultures."

"I wonder why he's even bothering doing this tour . . ." she said, half to herself.

"He still needs the voters behind him. A fickle lot, too. He's inching up in the polls, but it's not over yet," Leo reminded her. "Truthfully, all this razzle-dazzle is well and good. But in the long run he's got to take Boston. He's going to have to spend a lot more time canvassing Boston if he's going to pull this election out of the bag."

Catlin nodded. Leo was right. Most of the votes, most of the population lived in the greater metropolitan area of Boston. The election was still a horse race. The bus started moving and she closed her eyes and settled back for the ride to Gloucester. She would see even less of Matthew on this tour than she had on the last one. *Oh well*, she mused. *Perhaps it's just as well*. . . .

Gloucester was three centuries of weathered seafarers. It was majestic windjammers, whaling schooners, brine-soaked fishing nets. Over the three hundred years, ten thousand townsmen had been lost to the merciless depths of the sea. But the men still fished, as had their grandfathers . . . and their grandfathers before them . . . weaving their boats through the treacherous fog-shrouded shoals out, out to the sea, the dark blue eternal sea.

The invigorating smell of the salt air made Catlin feel buoyant and refreshed. The city was quaint and picturesque, dotted with weather-beaten clapboard homes, shingle roofs, antique shops, and lofty spires. She saw old homes, their windowed eyes looking ever seaward; their widow's walks still echoing from the restless vigils of long-dead women watching for their men to come home from the sea.

She saw churches, time-worn and stately, where countless prayers had been offered up for angelic protection for sailors and loved ones. She visited museums filled with ship models, period rooms, antiques, and old glass. And she watched Matthew Carr walk down the streets and wharfs, through the parks and public buildings walking, listening, meeting the people.

Everywhere he went he was followed by newsmen, reporters, cameramen. Everything he did was captured on film and tape and in photographs. He was surrounded—by the media, by the people, by the rigors of his campaign schedule. She did the best she could on her own reports for WTSB, but she found she was sending back more shots of locales than of the candidate.

She visited the Rocky Neck Art Colony alone, an artistic haven in the summer for writers and artists from all over the United States. She liked a large oil painting of a white sailing ship, heaving and tossing in the cobalt blue and white foam of the North Sea. She bought it for Taylor. She walked to the end of the street and stood on the gray granite rocks and watched the waves below hurl themselves against the rugged shoreline.

She empathized with them. It was exactly how she felt inside. Like she was helplessly beating herself against the constraints of her own nature. Her own standards. Her own loyalties. How simple her life had been before Matthew Carr and his rallying message of adherence to God's principles.

She read the Bible he had given her often, finding comfort there in the familiar stories and words of childhood Sunday school lessons. But she wasn't a child any more. Certain passages confused and disturbed her. Their meaning hovered on the edge of her understanding—like a song she could almost recall, but never quite recapture.

When the bus began its long, slow journey southward, taking Matthew to the people along the Massachusetts shoreline, Catlin rode, quiet and withdrawn. She had much to think about. . . .

Martha's Vineyard, accessible only by boat, was the playground of some of the state's oldest and most respected families. The Kennedy compound was there. So was the summer home of Van Cleef-Carr. The press had accommodations in various motels on the mainland. Matthew and his personal aides stayed at his sprawling home overlooking the beach and Nantucket Sound.

It was Fourth of July weekend when the entourage arrived. According to Matthew's agenda, he would stay in the area three days, delivering speeches and making appearances. He would spend the Fourth at a fund-raising cookout and then rest at his home before hitting the trail back to Boston the following day.

Catlin scanned the agenda sheet and felt renewed frustration. It would be impossible to get close to him for either personal or professional purposes. She could have gotten better tape footage if she had taken a network feed back at WTSB.

The Fourth dawned bright and beautiful. The sun beat white hot, highlighting the pinpoints of white sails on the blue water of the Bay. Mechanically she attended Matthew's news conference in Hyannis, sitting in the back of the American Legion hall, where she had gravitated naturally toward the network cameras, cables, and lights.

Leo sat next to her, his face its usual mask of boredom. She took a few notes, especially when one reporter tried to ridicule Matthew's "Back to the Bible" platform. But once the conference broke up, she decided she would return to her motel, get a lawn chair and spend the rest of the day soaking up the sun on the beach.

"Catlin?" She turned at the sound of her name and saw Dodd standing beside her.

She smiled. "How's May?"

"Fine," he said. She could tell he was in a hurry. "May's here. So is Lynda, Neal's wife. They're out at the summer house. Matthew's sorry he can't issue this invitation in person, but he hopes you'll understand."

"Invitation?"

"He wants you to join us this evening. At the house. We're going to have an old-fashioned clambake. Just us. Will you please come?"

Her heart thumped wildly. "I–I . . . why, yes. I'd love to come."

"Good!" Dodd's gray eyes softened. "You know we have the fund-raiser this afternoon, but May and Lynda will be at the house all day. Take the steamer over this afternoon." He spoke in quiet tones, and then as quickly as he had come, he was gone.

But the excitement he had brought lingered with her. An evening with Matthew! Suddenly, her lethargy left her. She bounced outside into the sweet, warm summer air, her mind whirling and spinning in anticipation of the evening to come.

were in Boston and in the summer home —

CHAPTER 7

CATLIN RETURNED TO HER MOTEL ROOM, showered,
washed her hair, and dressed carefully in white poplin
slacks, a bright green top, and sandals. She packed a
small tote bag with suntan lotion, a bathing suit, and
casual canvas shoes. She wanted to be prepared for
any activity. She applied her make-up artfully and
grabbed one last look in the mirror before she slipped
on sunglasses and a wide-brimmed hat.

She arrived at the summer home, stepped through
white gates, walked up onto the newly painted gray
wooden porch, and rang the doorbell. May opened the
door.

"Catlin!" The slender red-headed woman cried
with genuine pleasure. "Please come in. Dodd told me
you'd be coming."

Catlin followed the vivacious woman through the
sea breeze-cooled house toward the kitchen. This
house seemed so much friendlier than the huge,
foreboding estate back in Boston. It was bright and
cheery, decorated in white wicker, lime green, and
accents of teal blue. Large overhead fans stirred the

104

air gently, and expansive banks of paned windows looked out across a green sloping lawn that fanned out to a white sandy beach. Small white dunes rose in wind-rippled waves. Beyond the dunes lay the blue waters of the Bay.

"Lynda! Catlin's here!" May called to her friend as she entered the kitchen. Lynda turned from something she was doing at the sink and smiled a warm welcome.

"You're just in time to shuck the corn," the dark-haired woman said.

"Great! Just let me wash my hands," Catlin told her, eager to join in the hustle and bustle of kitchen work.

"The clams are already in the pit down on the beach," May said. "The men dug the pit and got everything started this morning before they left."

Catlin took her place next to Lynda and started ripping the green husks off the pale yellow ears of corn. May sat at a nearby table dicing cooked potatoes for potato salad.

"Where are the children?" Catlin asked, fondly remembering May's twin boys, and vaguely recalling the four smiling faces of Lynda's brood from the Easter picnic.

May and Lynda laughed in unison. "Back in Boston, parcelled out to friends and relatives. This is *our* special weekend. We plan to make the most of it!"

"Oh, they're such good kids," Catlin assured their mothers.

"You sound like Matthew," May said, wrinkling her nose. "Uncle Matthew loves having them underfoot. Honestly, he spoils them rotten. But this weekend is strictly for us grownups. We started coming down here for the Fourth a couple of years ago to plan campaign strategy. It got to be so much fun, we decided to make it a tradition."

"A tradition of swimming, clambakes and watching fireworks on the beach—*alone!*" Lynda added emphatically.

Catlin wondered who had spent the weekend with Matthew the year before. But she quickly shook off the jealous thought and concentrated on shucking the corn.

The afternoon passed quickly, and it seemed to Catlin that she had never had a better time. She discovered both women to be open and outgoing, easy to be with. At five, the men arrived.

"What a picture of domesticity!" Neal called out good-naturedly as he entered the kitchen.

"When do we eat?" Dodd asked, right on his heels.

Matthew entered last. Catlin looked up at him, almost shyly. A look of pure pleasure crossed his face at the sight of her. Her stomach fluttered as if she'd swallowed butterfly wings. "This suits you, Miss Burke," he teased and brushed her arm with his hand.

She thrilled at his touch. "Well, three-piece business suits don't suit a clambake!" she quipped.

The men changed hurriedly and then Neal and Matthew began toting the bowls, ice chests and hampers of food out the side door, across the lawn, over the dunes and down to the site of their feast.

Catlin changed into her swimsuit, slipped on a terry-cloth cover-up, and emerged into the kitchen in time to see Dodd tickling his wife. "Stop it," May shrieked between peals of laughter. She lunged for the kitchen faucet, got a handful of water and flicked it in his face.

"Now you'll pay!" Dodd warned. But May was too quick for him. She slipped from his grasp, bounded out the screen door, and dashed toward the water. Dodd pursued, laughing, and threatening her with retaliation.

Catlin strolled lazily along behind them, climbed over a small dune, and surveyed the beautiful blue

106

water. Gulls circled and called from overhead. The tangy, salt smell of the air always invigorated her.

Matthew walked to her, took her hand, his eyes never leaving her face. "Thank you for coming."

"Thank you for asking."

He enclosed her briefly in his arms, then left one arm draped across her shoulder. "Let's walk. I need to unwind and relax before I can concentrate on a party," he confessed.

"I'd love to." She clasped his hand, trudging through the soft sand, down toward the shoreline and splashed through the waves that ventured in to foam boldly against the wet sand.

"God must have rested here once He finished creating the universe," Matthew said thoughtfully. "I love this place. I always have. . . ."

"Sometimes . . ." Catlin started haltingly. "Sometimes I get so confused about where God fits into my life. . . ." She didn't mean for it to be a confession, merely an observation.

"Know what I think?" Matthew ventured.

She shook her head.

"I think you're being apprehended by Him."

"What?" She stopped short, thoroughly puzzled.

"Apprehended," he reiterated. "Chosen . . . for God's purposes."

She was skeptical. "I don't feel chosen," she said. "I feel confused about where I fit into the scheme of things."

He laughed gently. "I know the feeling." She hoped he would tell her more, open up his past to her. Instead, he said, "We all have a purpose in God's plan. Mine is politics. When it comes to doing His will, some of us go kicking and screaming . . . but we eventually go. Catlin," he turned his gaze from the water and stared down into the golden honey of her eyes, "sooner or later, you'll have to choose—between your way and His way."

Her way? She didn't understand what he meant. "I'm a TV journalist," she said, trying to make her tone light and sort out the impressions his words had left on her.

It made her uncomfortable, this talk of choosing. Why would God want her to choose between her career and His will? Besides, what was there to choose? She was good at her job. She reported stories factually and accurately. Hadn't she been careful so far to search out the truth about Matthew? Not to make snide implications about his life with Sandra? She knew of few reporters who would have been so solicitous.

"Faith," he stated simply. "It's letting go and trusting God to catch you."

Deep inside herself, she knew she couldn't do that. What if He wasn't there when she fell?

"I think this discussion has become far more complex than the day warrants," Matthew said with a smile on his lips. "Come on . . . let's go swimming."

Relieved, she tossed off her wrap and ran quickly into the water, calling to him, "Last one in is a lame duck!"

He plunged in behind her, sending a shower of sea spray into the air. They swam together in the cold, bracing surf, splashing and playing like children. "What would your public think if they could see you now?" Catlin teased over the lapping of the waves, determined to put their serious conversation behind her. "The political salvation of the state acting like a ten-year-old?"

"What would your viewers think," he tossed back at her, "if they could see TV's Wonder Woman splashing like a mermaid?"

Later, they left the water and raced along the shore in a game of tag football with Dodd, May, Neal, and Lynda. Once, Matthew spiraled the ball high over Dodd's head and Catlin caught it perfectly and sped for the end zone—two towels spread at the foot of the sand dune.

Much later, at the house, they showered off the salt brine, changed into casual clothes and went back down to the beach for their meal. There, in the rays of the setting sun, they feasted on warm salty clams, sugary sweet corn, May's creamy potato salad, rich chocolate brownies, and plenty of soda and lemonade.

Once darkness fell and the stars began to come out, the men built a small open bonfire. May produced marshmallows and Catlin held hers and Matthew's over the fire until they were toasty brown, singed only slightly around the edges.

"Delicious," he proclaimed, popping the gooey mess into his mouth. May and Dodd drifted off together in one direction down the beach; Neal and Lynda, in another. Catlin sat, her back resting against Matthew's broad chest, staring into the crackling fire, watching the red and orange and golden flames dance and shimmer in the velvet darkness.

Matthew's arm locked around her in a circle of warmth. He rubbed his cheek against her hair and then she felt his mouth glide across the nape of her neck, leaving small, soft kisses on the warm surface of her skin. Shivers of delight traveled up her spine, radiating down her limbs to the tips of her fingers.

"I'll give you an hour and a half to stop that," she whispered, trying to rouse herself from the spell of sensuous delight he was creating.

He chuckled and pulled her slightly closer to him. She was helpless, feeling herself rocked and lulled by his tenderness, by the respect in his tentative touch. Shamelessly, she wanted him to kiss her, hold her. She wanted to know everything about him—the gentle strength of his body, the secret recesses of his mind.

As Sandra had. . . . The thought stuck in her mind like a fishbone in her throat. *Forget* . . . she commanded herself. *Forget.*

109

Just then the sky erupted into a blaze of colored rain. "Look!" Matthew pointed. "The fireworks!"

Catlin watched, mesmerized, as showers of blue, red, green, and gold rained in sudden bursts and flashes. Quick, brilliant cascades of color, exploding and giving their brief moments of glory to the blackness of the sky.

"Beautiful . . ." she murmured.

"Yes . . . beautiful . . ." he echoed and turned her toward him, drawing her mouth against his, covering her pliant lips with a kiss that rivaled the fireworks above them. . . .

Summer's heat and humidity settled over the city of Boston, wilting the greenery of parks and lawns, drying up patches of the Charles River and firing the concrete and asphalt of the streets into furnaces. Nevertheless, with no respite from the weather in view, Matthew took his campaign to the people with frequent walking tours. He walked the city in sections, north to south, east to west, from the Boston Commons, past the State House, by King's Chapel, the Old North Church and Fanneuil Hall, meeting and greeting the people everywhere.

Catlin followed with the rest of the journalistic pack. But she kept her distance, both physically and emotionally. The Fourth of July weekend hung in her memory. She could not forget it. She could not deny it had happened. But she forced herself to think of her work, her job, her relationship with Taylor. Matthew didn't need her complicating his life throughout the remainder of his campaign. And she certainly didn't need him complicating hers!

Her feelings for Taylor had not changed. She lacked a consuming passion for him, but she felt a deep sense of loyalty to him. Their evenings together were comfortable at best. He took her out often. He had intimate dinners prepared for them at his lavish condominium. He doted on her. She shoved aside thoughts of Matthew, like bothersome intruders, intent on upending the orderliness of her life.

One hot August morning Maggie sauntered into Catlin's office, a mischievous grin spread across her large-boned features.

"You look like the cat that swallowed the canary," Catlin quipped. "What's up?"

Maggie's gravel voice was scratchier than usual. "Got some goodies for you, boss lady." Maggie handed Catlin a file folder. Curiously she thumbed through it. It was filled with photostatic copies from various police reports.

"Traffic citations," Maggie explained. "All on Sandra Carr. In fact, some go back a long time, even before she became Mrs. Carr. It seems Sandra liked to drive fast. Very fast. Wrecked two sports cars, got a suspended license once, paid a ransom in fines. . . ."

Catlin raised her eyebrows, and gave a low whistle. So the poor little rich girl had some flaws after all! "Daddy always bought her out, I suppose?"

"And after Daddy, Matthew," Maggie explained.

Catlin wasn't sure what it meant, but she was glad that Maggie had dug it up. "Good work, Maggie . . ." She flipped through the pile of police reports.

"It gets better." Maggie said conspiratorially.

"In what way?"

Maggie took the file and hand-picked several citations. "Lots are marked DUI," she informed Catlin.

"So she drank and drove . . . a lethal combination . . ." Catlin's voice took on an edge of sadness. "No wonder no one wants to talk about her. It's not a very pretty picture of one of Boston's elite."

Maggie leaned forward. "Yeah. But look at this." She laid out a series of copies on Catlin's desk. "These come closer and closer together. Especially after she became Mrs. Carr. Don't you see?" Maggie

111

asked excitedly. "Sandra was an increasingly unhappy woman. More and more tickets, more and more arrests, more and more booze. She must have been trying to escape *something* in her life.

"In fact," Maggie said after a brief pause, "the coroner's report shows that on the night she was killed, she was drunk, Catlin. Dead drunk."

The information did not set well with Catlin. It seemed that every time she picked up a rock in Matthew's life, something unpleasant crawled out. After five months, she didn't know much more about the "real" Matthew Carr than she had back in March. Once again, she felt thrust back to square one.

Catlin taped an "Inside" interview with Harold Cleaver. He had been demanding equal time for the extensive coverage WTSB had been giving to Matthew. Catlin disliked the current senator even more after spending a whole hour questioning him on the air. He was evasive and vague, impossible to pin down about specific issues and topics. He seemed oily and slippery to her.

"Good job." Taylor told her after viewing the tape in his office.

"The guy's a jerk!"

"Some choice, huh?" Taylor asked, pouring himself a tonic from his private bar. "We voters get to pick between a weasel like Cleaver, a deadbeat like Nolan, or a white knight with tarnished armor like Carr."

She bristled slightly. "I haven't uncovered any real tarnish yet," she reminded him. It was true. As unpleasant as the mystery of Sandra was to Catlin, Matthew had done nothing wrong or devious in his campaign.

Taylor leveled his gaze at her over the rim of his glass. "All his talk about the Banner of God blinding you?"

She bit her tongue. "I'm not foolish enough to attack God," she told him.

"Religion is for fools . . ." he said smugly. "Although even *I* have to admit that Carr has played it to the hilt. Used it for all it's worth. Take off your rose-colored glasses, Cat. Do your job," he demanded with cool fervor. "Every person is out for himself . . . Even Matthew Carr." He paused, then added, "*Especially* Matthew Carr."

She dropped her eyes. She honestly couldn't refute him. Not after the report from Maggie. Taylor set his glass down and came to her. He tugged her chin up and she looked up into his face. "I don't want to argue with you. Friends?"

She smiled wanly. "You're the boss . . ."

He dropped his eyes and his hand. "That's something else I want to talk to you about."

"I'm fired?"

"Hardly." He smiled beguilingly, glossing over their recent disagreement with a smooth, practiced air. "As you know, I'm heading out to Los Angeles in a few weeks for the fall programming extravaganza."

She knew. It was the annual ritual at TV stations all over the country. Station managers, public relations directors, owners and programming directors gathered yearly on the West Coast to preview the upcoming offerings from the various Hollywood studios and independent syndication houses. Taylor would be there for the purpose of buying new programming for WTSB viewers.

"Besides, I want to present some of the station personnel gathered there with an idea I've been formulating recently. And since it concerns you, I need to tell you about it."

Her interest piqued.

"I want to syndicate a talk show, Cat. A political show. Sort of like The Phil Donahue Show, but focusing exclusively on political interviews. It would present guests from all over the country, every marketplace, to talk about the political climate in America.'' She rolled the idea around in her mind. It did have potential. "And," he added, "I want *you* to host it.''

She gasped. "Me? B—But Taylor . . .''

He held up his hand to cut her off. "You'd be perfect. You're smart, politically savvy. . .and goodness knows, you're beautiful. You have it all, Catlin. Together, we'd make a great team. WTSB would produce the show. I'd pick up a distributor. I want to take some of your 'Inside' tapes and pieces you've been doing on Carr with me to L.A. I think I can sell the idea. One look at you, and they'll go for it. I'll bet you a dinner.'' He ended on a light note, sensing her turmoil.

Her own show in national syndication! Catlin reeled at the prospect. It was the dream of a lifetime. Taylor was offering her journalistic immortality. In some ways, it would be better than a move to a network.

"Don't panic!'' he laughed. "I've still got a lot of formulating to do on this idea. In fact, I've got a lot of formulating to do about *you*.'' His tone was kind, but secretive. "I want you to have dinner with me tonight,'' he urged. "There's something very special I want to show you.''

Catlin could only nod. A bright twinkle lit up his blue eyes. Grateful, and speechless, she rose on her tiptoes and kissed him. His arms tightened around her and he kissed her back with a sense of passion that startled her.

He released her, smiled, and stroked her cheek. "I'll pick you up at eight.''

Catlin walked back to her office in a state of utter confusion, excitement and anticipation. A national show! And she would be the star. What an opportunity he was giving her. How could she ever repay him? How could she ever thank him?

114

A package was waiting in her mail at the apartment when she arrived home from work, rushed and breathless. She had less than an hour to prepare for the special evening Taylor had promised her.

She ripped it open quickly, kicking off her shoes and starting her bath water at the same time. She paused long enough to lift the lid on the box, curious but slightly annoyed that it was demanding her attention. She lifted out the contents and heard her own breath escape in wonderment. It was a sea shell. A perfect chambered nautilus, polished and gleaming like a lovely jewel. A treasure from the sea. The insert card read: "I miss you. Matthew."

The shell caused a floodgate of memories to open and spill out across her mind. She remembered Matthew's touch, his arms around her, his brown eyes looking hard and deep into hers. "I miss you . . ." The words were almost audible. Her heart lurched, and something between sadness and wistfulness seized her emotions.

"I miss you. . . ." She ran her fingers over the smooth sand-colored surface of the shell. It was perfectly made, intricately formed; a flawless creation. Its internal chambers wound down within its interior, a tight and unique spiral that set it off from all other kinds of shells. Only God could have conceived such a shell, she told herself.

"I miss you. . . ." She remembered the smell of the sea, the feel of the sand beneath her feet, the dazzling display of fireworks in the night sky. Why would he remind her of that night with this gift? What did he want from her? It was too complicated. Too overwhelming for her to contemplate now. "I miss you. . . ."

She took a breath and silently slipped the exquisite shell back into its box. She gently laid the card beside it. Then she proceeded to dress for her date with Taylor.

She dressed elegantly, in a white crepe dress that fell in soft clinging folds from a band of sequins at her throat, leaving her shoulders and arms bare. She swept her hair up, in layers of auburn curls. Again, as on the night of the Charity Ball, the effect was calculated. She wanted Taylor to be proud of her, proud that he had chosen her for his project.

At eight o'clock, Taylor picked her up and they drove through the streets in the waning gray dusk. Twilight still lingered, a petulant child, reluctant to abandon her daylight playground to the night. Taylor was strangely silent, yet his eyes danced with excitement. She rode beside him, expectant and nervous, cushioned in the luxury of his car.

He drove her to his condominium, took a private elevator to the penthouse, then made her close her eyes as he led her out onto his patio overlooking the city. She opened her eyes on command and found herself standing in an arbor of flowers. "Taylor!" she gasped.

His entire patio had been transformed into a summer garden, greeting her eyes with a profusion of color and variety. Reds, purples, pinks, yellows . . . a symphony of color.

"Do you like it?" he asked, an uncharacteristic plea for approval tinging his voice. "I wanted tonight to be perfect."

"It's magnificent!" she murmured, turning in all directions, looking at the wonderland he had created for her. A table, intimately set for two, stood in the center of the garden. Candles glowed softly, their twin flames dancing in the dissipating twilight air.

The rich perfumes of the blossoms caused her to feel giddy. Her heart swelled with renewed tenderness and gratitude. "Thank you . . ." she whispered and slipped into his waiting arms. "It's so beautiful and so very thoughtful of you."

"I did it for you," he said. "I wanted the setting to be fitting."

She was mystified. "Tonight *is* special for me," she said softly. "You gave me a national TV show. . . ."

"There's one more thing. . . ." He produced a black velvet box from his coat pocket.

Her heart hammered and her fingers trembled as she took it from his outstretched palm.

"Open it."

She obeyed, mutely. Cradled on a bed of satin was a diamond of such exquisite beauty, of such magnificent fire that it took her breath away.

"I love you, Catlin," Taylor whispered into her ear. "Marry me. Be my wife."

CHAPTER 8

CATLIN STOOD FROZEN. unable to speak, gaping at the glittering stone in the soft candlelight. It was large and flawless. Its oval shape, its seemingly numberless facets, caught and refracted the candlelight, breaking the invisible spectrum into brilliant pinpoints of color. The stone seemed almost alive, shot through with rainbow lights, sparkling and glittering with a white fire.

"I–I don't know what to say . . ."

"Simple. Say yes."

Her eyes found his face. She swallowed hard. "Taylor . . . I–I . . . well . . . *marriage.*"

He dismissed her hesitation. "Surely, you know that I love you. . ."

"Yes . . . but marriage. . . ." The enormity of the commitment he was asking weighted her down.

"You do plan to get married some day, don't you?"

"Well, someday, yes. . . ."

"Let's see if it fits," he urged eagerly. He lifted the ring from its soft cushion, took her left hand, and slid it onto her third finger. It fit perfectly and gleamed with renewed life. He burst into a smile. "Perfection. It suits you."

She watched the diamond dance and sparkle on her hand. It *was* beautiful. He clasped both her hands in his and brought them to his lips, pressing a kiss across her fingers. "I want to marry you, Cat. I've known many women. I've even loved a few of them. . . ." He held her eyes with his own. "But you're the one I want to marry."

Her heart hammered, thudding and thumping against her ribs. Marriage . . . such a big step. A serious step. She *did* love Taylor—but enough to marry him?

Sensing her reticence, he continued. "I'll always love you, Cat. And I know that, given time and togetherness, you'll love me, too."

"Oh, I *do* love you," she cried quickly.

He smiled, a smile of understanding. "We'll be good together. Believe me. Keep the ring. Get used to the idea."

She wanted so much to please him, wanted so much to make him happy. But marriage. An act of commitment for all time. It wasn't something a person tried on, like a pair of shoes. She wasn't one to make vows lightly. Once she got married, she planned to stay that way.

Her emotions welled and crashed in her heart. Her head spun. Taylor pulled her against his broad chest. "Catlin Shentell . . ." he mused aloud. "It sounds right. Say yes, Cat."

Numbly, she nodded. "Yes, Taylor," she whispered. "I'll marry you. . . ." His embrace tightened and she stood motionless and somehow frightened. She closed her eyes. *I wish I could talk to Matthew.* . . .Then she stood, stricken by the impact of her wish.

119

Being engaged felt odd and cumbersome to Catlin. A little like carrying around an unfamiliar burden. Yet Taylor was like a man possessed. He was euphoric, attacking his work and his life with renewed passion and vigor.

He made her promise not to mention the engagement until the station employee party. "They're my family," he told her. "I want them to hear the news first, before the gossip columnists get hold of it."

In principle, she agreed that their co-workers should be the first to know. She would put off calling her parents until after the party. But every time the thought of Matthew's hearing the news crept into her consciousness, she quickly shoved it away. *I owe him no explanations!* she told herself fiercely.

The Saturday of the annual station party arrived, hot and muggy. Catlin had never looked forward to it, but her reluctance this year seemed more pronounced than ever. Every staff member and his family was expected to attend. There would be a cookout and a schedule full of games and activities. And Catlin knew that she would be required to be at Taylor's side every minute of the day, waiting for him to announce their engagement.

The station personnel gathered on the beautifully landscaped grounds of WTSB, beneath maples, oaks, and sycamores. Leaves hung limp and listless. A skeleton crew of engineers would keep the stations on the air, since most of the programming was pretaped or filmed. The proximity of the party allowed even these workers to join the festivities at staggered intervals.

Catlin dressed in white bermuda shorts that showed off her long, graceful, tanned legs. She chose a brightly flowered top that tied above her waist and white string sandals. The casual Caribbean look was completed with the addition of a scarf that lifted her heavy auburn hair off her shoulders. She looked fresh, vital, young.

Taylor had also dressed in white bermuda shorts, topped with a polo shirt in a cool shade of pale blue that matched his eyes exactly. With his silvered hair and rugged features, he was the picture of a handsome, cultured, continental.

Catlin mingled with her fellow workers, tense and controlled, the weight of Taylor's impending announcement heavy on her mind. What would they think? How many would be surprised? She had heard the gossip and rumors, conscious of the catty innuendoes and snide remarks about her meteoric rise to power and prestige at WTSB. She had always been able to shrug them off. But now. . . .

Why couldn't she be totally happy about her engagement? Why couldn't she just think like a dewy-eyed bride instead of a hard-headed reporter?

"You look preoccupied," Maggie said during a softball game pitting the executives against the work crew.

Catlin gave her a half smile. "I have a headache." It was an honest confession.

Maggie nodded in sympathetic understanding. "I know the feeling."

After the game, large ice-laden washtubs of cold watermelon appeared, and everyone took slices of the succulent, red fruit and lounged in more subdued clusters about the grounds. The heat and humidity, combined with unaccustomed activity, were taking their toll.

By the time Taylor gathered everyone for his closing remarks, dusk had moved in and the sun was sending red streaks across the sky. Catlin stood next to Taylor and watched him greet and praise his employees, like a benevolent father beaming over a brood of children.

"Lastly," he announced after a short pep talk about higher ratings, fall programming, and renewed dedication to WTSB, "I want to share some very special news with you."

He put his arm protectively around Catlin's shoulders. Her heart thudded. All eyes focused on her. "I've asked Catlin Burke to marry me," Taylor said, ". . . and she's agreed."

There was a moment of stunned silence, than an eruption of whispers and buzzing and finally a few handclaps that spread into a general applause. Taylor beamed at her and his employees. Catlin looked out at the sea of faces and smiled a bit too brightly.

She saw Ken Anderson's face first. He was clapping, but the look on his face was one of grim resignation. She shivered at the accusatory glare in his eyes and flushed under the implication.

"When's the big day?" someone called out from the crowd.

"As soon as we can set it," Taylor called back and gave her shoulders an extra squeeze.

Her eyes flew to him in bewilderment. Why would he say that? They had never even discussed a date for the wedding! She felt her anger flare. How typical of him to order her life as easily as he set a business agenda. "Taylor . . ." she interrupted.

He glanced down at her and smiled broadly. "The sooner the better," he announced loudly, ignoring the plea in her eyes. Then he kissed her lightly for the benefit of the crowd. They surged forward to congratulate the couple while she swallowed the bitter dregs of anger and resentment.

The gossip columnists broke the story in the Sunday morning paper. Natalie Hartford referred to Catlin as ". . . having landed *the* catch of the year," as if Taylor were some kind of fish she had been trolling for.

Catlin received so many congratulatory phone calls that she turned off her phone by mid-afternoon. She had ulterior motives for shutting off the constantly ringing phone, however. She was afraid that one of the callers might be Matthew.

122

Matthew. Every time her mind turned to him, it welled with confusion and doubt. What would he say to her? What would she say to him? Hoping to find refuge from her thoughts, she picked up the Bible he had given her, trying to recapture the peace she had often found inside. But she couldn't. The print squirmed on the pages and the words refused to make sense.

Taylor arrived at six o'clock and took her out to dinner. People who had read the gossip column intruded on the intimacy of their dinner with questions about the wedding. Catlin hated it. She just wanted peace and quiet. Sensing her tension, Taylor shortened the evening and took her home early.

"It'll die down," he assured her. "By tomorrow, the campaign will be back in the news and we'll be relegated to the back pages."

The campaign! She still had to follow the campaign. Matthew's campaign. With a deep sigh, she locked the door after Taylor had left and went to bed, more tired and drained than she had felt in years. . . .

Catlin drove slowly through the sun-dappled hills. In a few minutes she would arrive at the Van Cleef-Carr estate for the media luncheon planned especially for the social columnists, talk show hostesses and newspaper supplement magazines.

She had almost said no when May Brighton had called and asked her personally. It really wasn't that newsworthy an event. But May's gentle voice and gracious invitation were too much for Catlin to refuse. Besides, Catlin knew she would have to face Matthew's friends sooner or later.

She turned the WTSB newscar through the open iron gates of the property and drove cautiously up the tree-lined driveway. She had guessed right, back in April, when she had come that first time. The full foliage of summer *did* obscure the house from the foot of the long driveway.

She drove between the columns of trees, feeling their cooling shade, watching as the sun made flickering patterns through the branches. Splotches of light and shadow spilled onto the hood of her car. When she arrived at the crest of the driveway, the reality of the great house loomed, portentous, against the blue summer sky.

"Park your car?" a bright-faced young man asked through her car window. "We're putting all the vehicles down at the garage building," he explained. "Whenever you want to leave, I'll bring it up to you."

She handed him the keys and got out reluctantly, taking a few minutes to let her eyes wander over the impressive façade of the house and to collect her thoughts. She smoothed her bright green linen skirt and took a deep breath. She knew she was late, but she felt powerless to hurry her pace.

With feelings that vaulted between anticipation and dread, she walked up onto the veranda and rang the doorbell. A maid answered, took her special invitation, and directed her around the end of the veranda and out onto the back patio, where a large latticed gazebo perched picturesquely on the green, sloping lawn.

There, about fifty hand-picked women, reporters and journalists were seated, dining on fresh fruit salad. She recognized many of them from news conferences, newspaper photos and trade events—including the virulent Natalie Hartford. Catlin vowed silently to stay as far away as possible from the woman. Heads turned at her arrival, but it was the petite May Brighton who came over to her side.

"Catlin," May smiled graciously, "I'm so glad you came." There was no mistaking the sincerity and pleasure in her voice. Catlin let May take her hand and lead her to her appointed seat. May's hand brushed against the hard protruding diamond on Catlin's finger.

124

She glanced at the ring and said, "It's lovely." Yet her large blue eyes looked subdued and somehow a bit sad.

Catlin steeled herself and mumbled a polite "Thank you."

Once seated, Catlin turned to May and forced herself to speak brightly. "This is such a lovely idea. I know all of the women here are grateful for the opportunity to see this place."

"I hope so," May confessed. "Actually, it's my own little brainchild. Everywhere Matthew goes, someone asks about this house. It's so old, so steeped in tradition that I persuaded him to let me throw a luncheon—just for the local media people. Several are doing feature stories in upcoming editions of their papers. I've only allowed one photographer to attend, however. I didn't want it to turn into a circus."

"Will . . . will Matthew be here later?" Catlin asked as casually as she could. She had already observed that he wasn't present.

May shrugged. "I don't know." She gave the ring an involuntary glance. "I guess I'd better let you eat. I'll be conducting a tour of the main house and grounds later. See you then."

Catlin watched as May floated from table to table, greeting groups of women, listening to comments, accepting compliments. Catlin sighed and proceeded with the meal. The food was delicious, an elegant serving of cold soup, green salad, tasty shrimp salad and chocolate éclairs, presented on antique glass plates and dishes. She had little appetite, so she ate sparingly.

She followed the tour May conducted, only half-listening to the litany of historical facts surrounding the house's two-hundred-year heritage. She had toured it once before . . . with its owner. . . . Catlin shook her mind free of the memory.

Yet, as the small group of women clustered in the

marble foyer, Catlin's eyes strayed once more to the painting on the landing. It had not changed. Nor had its impact on her. Sandra Carr was still mistress of the house, just as surely as if she were alive in the room. It was her house. Her legacy. Her dream.

"Take a few minutes to look around," Catlin heard May say. "Then I'll take you all down to the formal gardens. They're quite lovely right now. The roses are in full bloom."

While the other women dispersed casually, exclaiming over the beautiful collection of Americana in the various rooms of the lower floor, Catlin continued to gaze at the disturbing portrait. She started when May appeared at her side.

"Did you know her?" Catlin asked.

"No," May confessed. "In fact, I didn't know Matthew until he started coming to our church several years ago. Lynda knew her though."

Catlin turned and looked at May with renewed interest. "What was she like?"

May chose her words carefully. "I understand from Lynda and Neal that Sandra was a bit . . ." May cast about for a word, ". . . wild," she finished. "Neal and Matthew were good friends in college. Neal was Matthew's favorite wide receiver on the football team," she explained. "He and Lynda double-dated with Matthew and Sandra a few times. Of course, Matthew was different then, too. He wasn't a Christian."

That surprised Catlin. It had never occurred to her that Matthew hadn't always been a vocal, active Christian.

"According to Lynda, Sandra was pretty possessive of him and a bit of a handful," May added with a slight laugh. "Evidently, after he married her, Matthew and Neal lost touch for many years. I really don't know much more." She lifted her gaze to the portrait once more. "She always looks so sad to me."

Catlin agreed silently. Apparently it was not her imagination. Sandra Carr looked sad because she had been a sad woman.

May led the group from the main house down a tree-lined footpath strewn with wood chips to a garden at the west end of the estate property. The sweet scent of hundreds of summer roses summoned the guests down the winding intricate pathways. All marveled at the artful display of splendid flowers.

Catlin reached out and let her fingers trail over the petals of one particular rose. It was a magnificent flower, as large as a saucer, pale lavender in color and velvet soft to her touch. "Lovely, isn't it?" a woman's voice asked.

Catlin turned to encounter the appraising eyes of Natalie Hartford, social busybody for Boston's biggest newspaper. Catlin nodded, and then hurried off to lose herself in a group of women. She couldn't face Natalie and her prying eyes and acid tongue. Not today.

After the tour of the garden, May led the women back to the house and into the formal dining room, where a silver coffee service had been set. Clusters of delicate bone china cups, pastry puffs and mints beckoned invitingly. "Feel free to visit for a while in the formal parlor," May invited. "Linger as long as you like."

Catlin allowed herself to relax, absorbing the genteel elegance of that wonderful dining room. How lovely it was! This time, the bright rays of the summer sun shimmering through the voile curtains acted like a veil, shutting out time and making the room a refuge from the present.

Accepting a cup of coffee from a uniformed maid, she drifted into the parlor and scanned the small groups of women. She felt shut out, apart, cut off. May was busy with her hostess duties, so Catlin took her cup and stepped out onto the fan-cooled veranda. She let her eyes roam the green lawns.

"Congratulations, Miss Burke." Matthew's voice came from behind her and the cup rattled in her hand, causing her coffee to spill into the saucer. She turned to face him, forcing a smile to her lips.

He stood gazing at her, his hands thrust in his pants pockets, his silk dress shirt open at the neck. His eyes were cool, guarded and wary. A muscle, tensing in his jawline, gave a clue that he was exerting massive self control.

"Thank you . . ." she said stiffly.

"I had no idea that you and Taylor Shentell were so . . . close." His tone was low and deliberate; his eyes, relentlessly penetrating.

She couldn't bear the look in those eyes, though she couldn't define it, so she dropped her head and stared into the black liquid of the coffee cup. "I–I was taken by surprise, too . . ." she managed weakly. It was harder to face him than she had ever imagined. But why? They had no ties. They had made no promises. Taylor loved her. He wanted her. . . .

"Marriage is a lifetime commitment," Matthew said. "It's a covenant, under God." Spoken in that somber tone, the words sounded like both a warning and a chastisement.

She felt color rise to her cheeks and a biting retort to her tongue: "Unless some act of God relieves you of your commitment."

He received her words like blows and she regretted them instantly. "May you be happy," he said softly.

She wanted to reach out to him, longed to say, "I'm sorry. Forgive me!" But she just stood, mute, hot tears pricking at her eyes, and watched him turn and move toward the doorway, toward the roomful of women who were eagerly awaiting his arrival.

Catlin sighed deeply and set her cup down on the veranda railing. She turned to leave, but she found her path blocked by Natalie Hartford, her eyes probing and narrowed, her expression both knowing and speculative.

"Excuse me!" Catlin said brusquely and darted past the woman. She hurried down the steps of the veranda, to the driveway. She wanted to get away. Away from the party, the people, the atmosphere. But mostly, she wanted to get away from the house. The vast and lonely house . . . and the strange melancholy shadow of its former mistress.

"What do you think, Cat? I like that segment. Do you?" Taylor spoke from his seat in the director's booth, overlooking the console and banks of TV monitors.

Catlin nodded, her eyes scrutinizing her own image, frozen and framed on the screen. "Yes, that piece is fine," she agreed.

"We'll take it, Larry," Taylor said to the director who sat at the console, his fingers on the control panel, and its banks of buttons, levers and switches.

Larry relayed the necessary information through his headset to the engineer in master control and waited while the clip was transferred to the master tape Taylor and Catlin were building.

Catlin was tired. Her eyes stung from the strain of watching the monitor screen so intensely. The muscles at the base of her neck felt tight and sore. They had been working for three straight hours—painstaking, tedious hours—and it might be that many more before Taylor found what he was looking for in the hundreds of "Inside" tapes, news reports and footage of Catlin doing her job.

Taylor would be leaving for Los Angeles on Thursday, only a few days away. He wanted a perfect tape to show the gathering of TV people on the West Coast. A great tape capable of convincing them that Taylor's idea of a syndicated political talk-show was an idea ripe and ready for the mass audience. And that Catlin Burke was the perfect vehicle to implement that idea.

At the end of the work session, they would have a thirty-minute tape to show prospective buyers. It was already partially scripted. Catlin had written it and Taylor had approved the script. Now, all that remained was to select the best tape segments, edit a master, and insert the necessary special effects in the director's booth to make it look slick, professional, and dynamic. It all hinged on Taylor's ability to sell it.

She had little doubt that he would. It had become a fixation with him, this idea of his. Personally, she felt both anxious and hesitant. It would be a tremendous responsibility to take on a full-time show. It would also take a lot of capital. And how would all of it affect her ability to be a wife? To be under Taylor's watchful, husbandly eye all the time?

Other couples did it. She knew of several highly successful husband and wife creative teams. But could she do it? Especially when she wasn't even sure she wanted to be a wife?

"Tired?" Taylor asked. Without waiting for an answer, he reached over and kneaded the muscles of her neck with firm strokes. She felt the muscles relax under his ministrations.

"I think we'll quit for a while, Larry," Taylor told the portly director.

"No . . ." she protested.

"We can wrap it up tomorrow," he insisted. "There's not too much left to do, and besides we'll be fresher then. Now come on back to my office and let me fix you something."

She agreed and they left the booth and walked through the cold silent studio. Catlin shivered. It was ten o'clock. In an hour, the crew would set up for the eleven o'clock news show, but now the studio was deserted and empty and cold. It was always cold. Once the banks of lights came on, however, sending down their searing heat rays, the staff would welcome the extra coolness.

130

In Taylor's office, she kicked off her shoes and fell onto his sofa.

He grinned down at her fondly. "What do you want?" he asked. "Coffee, tea, or me?"

"Iced tea," she replied, ignoring his small joke. She scanned the scattering of papers that covered the coffee table next to the sofa while he went to the bar and clunked large cubes of ice into a frosted glass.

"I see you have the results of the latest election polls," she said casually. "I'm too tired to read them. What do they say?"

"That Matthew Carr is gaining fast," he said somewhat grimly. Her pulse quickened at the news. Taylor continued, "Of course, Cleaver still controls organized labor and most of the feminist groups. But Carr certainly has eroded his base with the man on the street. . . ." Taylor brought her the glass of tea and then settled next to her on the sofa.

"I can't get over how that guy's caught on with the people. What were our forefathers thinking about when they left the election process in the hands of the common man?" Taylor mused condescendingly. "It looks like Nolan is finished. He hasn't got the money or the manpower. Even his own party is writing him off."

Catlin sipped the minty tea. It was immensely refreshing. "Well," she commented, "Carr's climbing rapidly, but the election's only two months away. After Labor Day, he's planning another swing through the state. That may push him over the top."

"Whose side are you on anyway?" Taylor asked sharply.

"I'm impartial, remember?" She skirted his question.

"Can you imagine having that guy shaping policy for this country? The thought makes me shudder."

She knew she should be siding with Taylor. After all, she was going to marry him. But she couldn't

131

pretend to share his beliefs when, both personally and politically, she felt that Matthew Carr would be an asset to the country. He was a man of conviction and principle. He believed in God and in God's divine purposes for the country. She smiled inwardly. No . . . Taylor would never understand it. Never. Because he didn't understand God. And somehow, she knew he never would. Religion was foolishness to Taylor. A waste of time.

While she didn't have the relationship with God that Matthew had, she did believe in Him. And that simple belief was like a fissure between her and Taylor, a crack that ran across the crust of their relationship. How long would she be able to maintain her search for a closer union with the Lord once she was Taylor's wife? How long before the pressures of her husband's lifestyle pulled her farther and farther from a desire to know Him?

The ring on her finger struck the side of the glass she held, and the stone caught her eye. The diamond blinked back at her. Hard and cold and lifeless.

Catlin sank low into her pillow and groaned. Her head throbbed and her throat felt so raw and sore she could hardly swallow. She shook down the thermometer from the glass on the bedside table and slid it under her tongue. Then she lay back and counted the long moments by the regular pounding of her head. She removed the thermometer and squinted between the surges of pain at the fine red line: 102 degrees.

"Terrific . . ." she mumbled. This was the morning Taylor was leaving for L.A., and she couldn't even stagger to the station to see him off to the airport. She managed to get to her bathroom and fumbled around in the medicine cabinet for aspirin. She washed three tablets down with gulps of water and got back under the covers, her teeth chattering with chills.

The phone rang on her bedside table and she jerked

132

it up to silence it. "Hello, beautiful!" Taylor's cheerful voice greeted her. "Feeling any better?"

"I'd have to die to feel better," she moaned.

"I told you last night you were catching something," Taylor said reproachfully.

"I did just what you said. I took aspirin, hot tea, and went straight to bed."

"Look, honey," he started. "I hate to leave you when you're sick. But I've got to go to these meetings. . . ."

"Be serious," she chided. "It's just the flu. Not worth canceling your trip over. I'll be fine."

"What's on your docket today?"

Her agenda! With a start, she realized that this was the day of Matthew's luncheon speech in downtown Boston. She was scheduled to cover it with Red. "The Carr luncheon . . ." she told Taylor. "It's a big one. He and Cleaver on the dais together."

"I'll send Ken," Taylor told her. "Sue can tag along, too. Now, as for you," he added, "get some rest. Sleep away the day; don't come in tomorrow either. Relax this weekend. I'll be back Monday night, expecting you to be well and rested."

"Thanks, Taylor." She knew he would parcel out her duties and clear her work schedule. She regretted missing the political luncheon—mostly because she wouldn't be able to see Matthew. A perversely persistent part of her still missed him very much.

"Take care of yourself," Taylor's voice came to her over the receiver. "If you want, call my personal physician. He'll fix you up with some of those fancy wonder drugs."

"I'll be fine."

"I love you, and I'll see you Monday night. Maybe we'll have something to celebrate." His voice was vibrant with anticipation.

After she hung up, Catlin closed her eyes and pulled the covers up over her head. She considered taking

133

her phone off the hook, but decided against it. In a few minutes, she fell into a leaden sleep.

From far away, a persistent ringing sound beat against her wall of unconsciousness. She rose out of the deep stupor of sleep like a swimmer rising to the surface of a pool. She could almost see the daylight above her and struggled for it as if her lungs were bursting for air. She felt herself crashing to the surface and gasped lungfuls of fresh air, then realized that she was awake and that the ringing sound was her phone, not a sea bell.

She grabbed the offending receiver. "Hello . . ." she mumbled, annoyed at the intrusion, yet relieved that she felt better. Her head wasn't pounding, and the fever must be down because the chills were gone.

"Catlin?" It was the tense, breathless voice of Sue Davis.

Instantly Catlin was wide awake, her nerve endings tingling.

"Catlin?" Sue asked. "Have you had the TV or radio on?"

"I've been asleep . . ." Catlin said, confused and alarmed.

"Then you'd better turn it on," Sue said tightly. "Some lunatic just shot Matthew Carr!"

CHAPTER 9

T̶H̶E AUDITORIUM OF THE HOSPITAL, housing a make-shift press conference, was filled to overflowing—packed, crammed, bulging with reporters and journalists, their cameras and equipment in tow. The room buzzed with voices, and the atmosphere crackled, heavy with rumor and speculation.

Matthew Carr was still in the emergency room. There was no true information on his condition, no facts to support the predictions.

"He's dead."

"Naw . . . the bullet never touched him."

"I heard he's just barely alive."

Catlin stood dizzily in the crowd, and waited with the rest of them for the next news release. She was too numb to acknowledge colleagues, too stunned to talk or think or feel. She was in the dark like all the others. A hard, solid lump of fear sat in her stomach like a fist, and a sensation of cold, clammy horror engulfed her. Her lungs felt constricted in her breast and she had to will her feet to move and her tongue to respond to even the simplest of questions.

The auditorium had been set up for the media; soon doctors would come to tell them what they were all waiting to hear. Police had completely sealed off the ER area of the hospital, and their blue coats could be seen everywhere. But there was still no news. No news. . . .

For every reporter inside the auditorium, two more waited outside the hospital—in the lobby, the parking lots, the streets. Those inside were part of a reporter pool, a lucky number who had been chosen to attend the conference. Ken Anderson was supposed to be there, but Catlin had pulled rank on him.

"You can't!" he had blurted in heated anger.

But the look she had given him had stopped his outburst. She was *going* inside. And God help Ken if he tried to stop her. So now, she waited . . . and every minute was agony, a purgatory of anguish that tore and ripped at her insides like a ravenous wolf.

Matthew Carr had been shot on the sidewalk— while throngs of well-wishers gathered around him; while demonstrators protested his politics and carried picket signs against him; while security personnel, friends, acquaintances stood all around him; while he waited for his car to whisk him away to yet another meeting. In the white-hot heat of the dog days of August, on a Boston sidewalk, a man had stepped forward from the bowels of the crowd. He had raised a handgun, aimed it only momentarily, and fired. Point blank. Straight at Matthew.

"It sounded like a pop gun," Sue had remarked. "Like a toy."

And Matthew had fallen. "He was shoved," said one witness. "He was knocked down by the bullet," said another.

Security people had formed a ring around him. And the police had drawn pistols. And the crowds had screamed and scattered. And the ambulance had come, taking him away . . . away to this place, this edifice of healing. This place of doctors and machines and drugs. And still, two hours later, there was no word. No news. No facts. Catlin thought she would go mad with the waiting.

She tried to pray. Tried to plead with God for Matthew's life. Tried to bargain with the Creator for this one man; this one human being. But all she could do was clench her fists, squeeze her eyes shut and whisper, "Please. . . ."

When the door of the auditorium opened and a man entered, a low, anticipatory murmur shot through the room. The man walked briskly, with authority, to the stage and the podium spiked with microphones.

"I'm Detective Kiefer," the dark-haired man announced. "Dr. Malone will be here shortly with news about Mr. Carr." A moan of disappointment rumbled through the gathering. "But I do want to assure you that the perpetrator of the crime is in custody. At this time, we have no reason to believe that he was part of a conspiracy. We are convinced that he acted entirely on his own and with malice aforethought."

Another wave of conversation rippled through the audience. "Malice aforethought. . . ." Catlin knew the phrase meant one thing and one thing only. The man had meant to shoot Matthew. He had planned it.

"You have his confession?" a reporter called out.

"We do," Kiefer affirmed with a nod, then he held up his hand to shut off the deluge of questions that erupted.

Simultaneously, a white-coated physician entered the room. His lab coat looked fresh and crisp, but Catlin noticed flecks of blood on his trousers legs. The fear welled up again, sending waves of nausea through her.

"I'm Dr. Malone," the sandy-haired man intoned, stepping up to the microphones. "I've just operated on Matthew Carr."

For a few moments, bedlam rocked the crowd.

Catlin shut her ears to the wall of noise and tried to focus what was left of her sanity on the doctor at the podium. He turned swiftly and lowered a chart from the ceiling over the stage. It was an anatomy drawing.

"The bullet entered Mr. Carr's shoulder . . . here," the physician continued, pointing to the drawing. "It lodged here . . ." he pointed again ". . . and I removed it thirty minutes ago.

"His life is not in danger," the doctor announced above the rumble of voices. "He's alive and I expect a full recovery. We will be keeping him here for observation and issuing updates on his progress every four hours. I will now take your questions."

Voices erupted all around Catlin as reporters began to call out questions, each attempting to outshout the next one. Catlin leaned against the wall for support, her knees suddenly feeling weak and rubbery. For the first time, she glanced down at the palms of her hands, surprised to see blood where she had dug her nails into them.

For Catlin, the second phase of her agony was knowing that she couldn't get to Matthew. She had no privileges, no special authority, no means at her disposal that would gain her access to his room. Her desire to see him, touch him, speak to him, was almost physical. She wanted to see for herself that he was all right—that no one had lied. She wanted to hear from his own lips that he was fine.

She did not sleep that night. The next day at the hospital, she waited again for the periodic updates. They were short and simple. Condition: satisfactory. She could not get through to either Neal or Dodd and, by Saturday morning, her intuition told her that Matthew was no longer at the hospital.

May! The inspiration came to Catlin in a flash. May Brighton would help her reach Matthew. She *had* to! Catlin found the Brighton house on a quiet street in

138

Arlington, among a row of similar houses. It was an older home, renovated in white clapboard with Cape Cod shutters and a white picket fence.

May came to the screen door, wiping her flour-covered hands on her apron, and gasped with surprise and pleasure to see Catlin. She brought her into the house, past a staircase, down a narrow hall with polished oak floors to a kitchen, sunny and bright, and filled with the aroma of freshly baking bread.

Her twins sat, occupied with clay, at a small table at one end of the rambling kitchen. May's countertops were strewn with bowls, a giant mixer, flour, measuring spoons, and a large wooden kneading board. "I have to do something to keep my mind occupied," she explained waving her hands toward the clutter.

"I have to see him, May," Catlin pleaded, her anguish filling her golden eyes. "Please, help me. I–I know he's not here. I know he's not at the hospital. But you know where he is. I know you do."

May looked at Catlin for a long moment, her own soft features absorbing Catlin's heart cry. "He's in the Bahamas. Neal and Dodd are with him. Let me make some calls," she offered gently and added, "He is all right. Dodd made him go for a few days rest. But he really is all right."

Catlin squeezed her eyes shut to force back their misting veil. "Thank you . . ." she whispered.

May brushed her arm with a touch of womanly understanding. "Can you stay with the boys for a few minutes while I call?" Catlin nodded. "You remember Miss Burke, don't you, boys?"

The set of identical faces looked up at Catlin, wide-eyed. "This is Sean and this is Erik." Catlin noted Sean was on the right. If they moved she would never be able to tell one from the other. "Now behave," their mother admonished and, wiping her hands again, she left the kitchen.

"You're the lady on the news," Sean announced. "I watch you."

"That's not so," his brother objected. "Uncle Matthew watches you."

Sean glared at his brother and snapped, "Well, I watch her, too!"

Catlin smiled and dropped down to her knees at their small table. "What are you making?" Their busy fingers kept rolling and pounding the clay into neat little strips and balls and loops.

"Stuff . . ." Erik offered.

"Can I make some 'stuff,' too?"

"Sure!" Erik told her.

She picked up a lump of clay and rubbed it against her hands to make it pliable.

"Some bad man shot Uncle Matthew," Sean announced matter-of-factly.

Catlin felt her voice catch in her throat. "Y–Yes, I know. . . ."

"Mama says we have to pray for him."

"Both of them," Erik amended. "We got to pray for *both* of them. Uncle Matthew *and* the bad man."

Catlin swallowed a lump in her throat, trying hard to tighten the rein on her emotions. *Pray for them.* "Forgive them, Father. They know not what they do. . . ." The familiar words of Christ flooded back to her.

May reentered the kitchen and Catlin rose to greet her. What if Matthew had said no? What if he didn't want to see her? For the first time, the thought struck her that he might never want to see her again.

May's smile washed the fear away. "Yes," she said, taking Catlin's hands in her own. "Matthew wants to see you very much. Once you get to Freeport on Grand Bahama, call this number." May handed her a slip of paper. "Dodd will pick you up."

The gratitude that filled Catlin made it almost impossible for her to speak. She sent her thanks by gripping May's hands tightly. "God bless you. . . ."

"And you too, Catlin," May whispered. "You, too."

Catlin packed lightly, in a shoulder tote bag. She dressed in white poplin slacks and a gauzy blouse with sleeves that rolled up and buttoned over the elbow. She covered her hair with a scarf and added dark glasses, intent on blending into the crowd of travelers at Logan Airport. She caught a noon flight to Miami International and, in Miami, managed to make a late afternoon plane for the Bahamas.

In Freeport, she called the number May had given her and felt relieved when Dodd's familiar voice greeted her. "I'll be there as soon as I can," he promised. He arrived, dressed casually in a Hawaiian print shirt, clasped her hand briefly, and led her to a nondescript car parked outside the terminal.

"I'll need to make reservations for the night somewhere," she told Dodd in the car.

"I've arranged for that already." He started the engine and eased into the airport traffic. "Right now, let's get to the house. We're staying at a friend's home," Dodd explained. "He winters here in a place on the west side of the island."

Dodd wove in and out of the traffic, and Catlin gazed at the colorful streets and shops of the island. It was already late afternoon, and many bicycles, pedestrians and tourists filled the narrow streetways, heading for home, hotels and the famous Bahamian night-life.

"It's good to see you," Dodd added. "This place where we're staying is secluded—private grounds, private beach—just what the doctor ordered. Matthew plans to spend a few days here, and then get back to Boston and pick up his campaign again."

"So soon after . . ." She couldn't bring herself to utter the words.

"He's healing nicely, and he can't afford to lose the momentum he's got going with the voters." Dodd grew quiet, then added, "It was a vicious act, by a disturbed person. We'll tighten security, but it's behind us. And we have to go on with the campaign."

141

They arrived at a private driveway where a security guard slid open a gate, allowing the car entrance through a wide, gravel path. Catlin was unprepared for the palatial size of the house and grounds—and the number of guards stationed at discreet intervals around the stucco mansion. It gleamed like a pink jewel against the blue sky, surrounded by clipped green lawns, hedges of hibiscus and trellises thick with white and purple bougainvillaea. The roof, low and Bahamian in design, shone brilliant and white in the sun.

"I'll take your bag," Dodd offered. "Matthew's down on the beach. And Catlin," he caught her arm, "I'm glad you came. You're good medicine for him. The experience—the hell of that gunman trying to kill him—well. . ." Dodd's voice trailed. "He needs someone like you right now."

She nodded, shuddering at the memory of her own anguish during the time she had waited for word on Matthew's chances for survival. With some kind of intuitive sixth sense, she understood how it must have been for Matthew. A man he had never met, a stranger, had tried to destroy him. For no reason at all.

She walked to the beach. The powdery white sand felt warm and soft on her sandals. She saw him at once, standing with his back to her, gazing out across the turquoise waters of the sea. Already the sun was slipping down the horizon toward the waiting, calm water as if it might float there, like a giant beach ball.

"Matthew. . . ." She called his name and he turned to face her. His left arm was in a black sling that covered his wounded shoulder. It stood out, like mourning, against his red polo shirt.

He held out his right hand and she slipped eagerly against his side, careful not to brush against his left shoulder. He bent his head downward and she instinctively lifted her lips to receive his. They came

142

down hungrily on hers, searching and warm. It was a long kiss of exquisite sweetness that made her feel like a flower opening itself to the sun. He pulled away slowly and gazed into her face. "You're really here . . ." he said as if her presence hadn't yet penetrated his consciousness.

Her tears came then, soft and cleansing, and she clung to him while the sun sank lower toward its rendezvous with the sea. "Let's sit here for a while," he suggested. "I just want to look at you."

He led her to a blanket spread out on the sand and pulled her down next to him. He made a resting place for her head against his raised knees and she leaned back and gazed up into his face. He ran the thumb of his right hand along her jawline, his eyes drinking in her loveliness.

"When I heard . . ." she began haltingly.

"Shh-shh . . . It's all over now."

The dying sun had colored the sky with flamingo and crimson, casting a warm glow over Matthew's features. But his eyes—his green-flecked, light brown eyes—never left her face. She raised her hand to touch his mouth with her fingertips, as if to reassure herself that he would not fade away in the final rays of the sun. The gesture proved to be a mistake.

The last light of the sinking sun hit the diamond on her finger and shot off pinpoints of fire—blinding, star glints of cold white fire. The muscles in his jaw tensed and he caught her hand, imprisoning it in his own, and stared at the twinkling stone. She shrank against him and guiltily tried to pull her hand free. The glow left his eyes, and confusion, then coolness and finally resignation settled there.

She had forgotten. For almost three days, she had totally forgotten about everything else in her life. About her engagement . . . her job . . . Taylor . . . Sandra. She had forgotten it all. Now the reality of that other life rushed back to her in the accusatory glimmer of a diamond solitaire ring.

Matthew pushed away from her, his expression unreadable. He stood and she scrambled to her feet beside him. Words formed in her throat, but she couldn't get them out.

Matthew spoke first, "What do you want from me, Catlin?"

She could not answer. She quickly erected her defenses. "I–I was worried. . . ." Her evasive answer sounded weak and hollow to her own ears.

"Perhaps you made a mistake coming here." The finality in his voice stung.

"Perhaps I did . . ." she agreed lifelessly.

He turned again and looked down at her. "Your heart," he said. "Where is your heart?"

She could not answer him, and she backed off mutely. He turned and walked quickly down the beach. She watched him go, feeling a part of herself go with him. Feeling like half of her had just drowned. Ironically, at that moment, the rim of the sun slipped into the sea.

She couldn't stay. She realized that at once. Feelings of frustration and loneliness consumed her. She had to leave. So she returned to the house and asked Dodd to take her back to the airport. Surprised, shocked, he agreed and in less than an hour, she sat waiting for a return flight to Miami at the Bahamian terminal. How brief. How futile. What had she accomplished by coming? She was no closer to Matthew than she had ever been. Something in her wanted him. But something else was afraid. Afraid to let go. Afraid to. . . .

By Monday, Catlin Burke had her life back under control again. She attended the WTSB news staff meeting. She performed her job. She greeted Taylor when he returned from Los Angeles.

"Lots of excitement, I hear," Taylor stated, waiting for her to settle next to him on the sofa in her living room. She served coffee and curled up beside him.

144

She delivered facts, giving him all she knew on Matthew's story. Her own involvement, her own desperation, her own flight to the Bahamas, she withheld. It wasn't part of the news story anyway. And it would have only hurt and angered Taylor.

After they talked, he gathered her into his arms and kissed her. "I missed you," he whispered. She closed her eyes and willed herself to concentrate on him. "I've got good news," he told her, brushing her hair with his lips. "Very good news. It looks like our news show is a go. Everyone who saw it liked it, and they *loved* you."

She smiled, forcing herself to be a part of his enthusiasm. *This will be enough,* she said to herself. *This is the life I'd planned anyway.* She would have Taylor and the TV show and she would be happy. And after the campaign . . . after the election . . . Matthew Carr would be out of her life forever.

Over the next few days, Catlin worked feverishly on a news piece about the attempted assassination. She created and produced the story, emphasizing the impact of the act on the overall Carr campaign. Ironically, in the long run, the attempt on his life strengthened his position with the voters, causing a backlash of outrage among both Christians and backers of Matthew's traditionalism values. The piece proved so dynamic and perceptive that the Independent Cable Network picked it up for national telecasting.

"He's going to win it," Taylor commented glumly one September afternoon. "I feel it in my gut. Somehow he's managed to dupe all these people. . . ." He dropped the results of the latest polls onto his office desk and Catlin watched him resume his pacing. "And now he's going to win it."

She scanned the papers he'd discarded. They revealed that Matthew had, indeed, pulled to within a few percentage points of Cleaver. And with the election only eight weeks away, Matthew did seem to be in a strong position.

Yet Taylor's attitude made her uneasy. She still could not comprehend why Matthew's steady rise to popularity with the voters rankled Taylor so much. But it did.

"Are you *sure* you've found nothing in his past to shed some light on his true colors?" Taylor asked her that same afternoon.

She shrugged. "Nothing."

"Wasn't there something with his wife? You mentioned her to me once before. You said that maybe there was something about the two of them . . ." He looked at her expectantly and, for the first time, she detected a decidedly unpleasant aspect to Taylor's countenance. There was a diabolical gleam in his eye, as if it were very important to him that she turn up something that would discredit Matthew.

"Nothing solid," she hedged, feeling uncomfortable. "Still nothing more than rumors and innuendo."

"Can't you do a piece on those rumors?"

Catlin stared at him. "Smear him with rumors? Really, Taylor, it's hardly my style!"

"You owe it to the public to give them information." Taylor grew agitated as they talked.

Catlin felt her own temper mount. "I owe it to the public to give them *facts*. I have no facts to link Matthew with anything spurious in his past."

"Matthew?" Taylor asked, eying her coldly over the familiar use of his first name.

Color flushed her cheeks. "Habit," she commented, "from hanging around his campaign."

He watched her for a few moments, as if evaluating something, then announced quietly, "You're not going on this final tour, Cat."

"What?" she asked incredulously, whirling to face him. "Taylor! You can't be serious! Not after all the time and effort I've put into this story."

146

"I want you here," he said with deliberate pause. "WTSB has given Carr too much air time already. His free ride is over. You're off the story and that's that. I still set policy around here, you know."

His words, his tone, his demeanor stung her. He was pulling her off the story and there was nothing she could say about it. Anger welled up. She struggled to maintain a grip on her volatile emotions. Realistically, she knew he was right. There really was no need for her to go on the tour. She would just be stumbling over network people again. But his method of telling her, of dictating and forcing her to do his will, left her boiling inside.

She wanted to fight with him about it, wanted just once to explode and tell him exactly how she felt about his domineering nature. But she knew that he would get angry and their clash would be violent. And in the end she would do exactly what he wanted anyway. Secretly, deep within her heart, she really didn't want to face Matthew again. Her feelings about him were too ambivalent.

"All right," she told Taylor crisply. "You're the boss."

"We have much to do on our own show," Taylor added, in a placating tone. He moved around in front of his desk and reached out for her. But she stepped backward, beyond his reach, and went swiftly to his office door.

"Later, Taylor," she said, "let's talk about it later. I'm really not up to it now." Then she left his office, her feelings still smarting under his dictatorial attitude.

"It's for the best," she mumbled to herself all the way back to her own office. *It'll all be over soon*, she told herself, realizing the full implication of her words. Taylor had pressed her to set a wedding date the night before. She had hedged.

"After the campaign . . ." she had told him reluctantly.

"December," he had told her with finality. "You'll make a beautiful winter bride."

She had gone into his arms, her heart pounding with apprehension. No, it didn't matter at all if she went on this last campaign tour with Matthew. Soon, the election would be over, and by Christmas, she would be Mrs. Taylor Shentell.

October came, and with it the banner of autumn. Catlin reveled in the welcomed change of the season. In some ways, this was her favorite time of the year. Crisp, sparkling, wind-nipped days and long frost-tipped nights spray painted the trees with russets and golds and yellow-oranges. Bright blue skies gave way to dark, blustery cloud banks. Canada geese filled the heavens with their V-shaped wedges, their forlorn cries filling her heart with renewed restlessness and longing.

Catlin moved through the days, distracted, busy, ever building toward the finality of November. She gave what she could to the campaign, hovering on the outer fringes of Matthew's activities, insulated behind the safety of her crew and camera. Sometimes, when she wasn't on guard, he would catch her eye and hold her gaze with the fathomless depths of his eyes. At these times, her heart pounded crazily. Nothing had changed—and everything had changed.

They spoke, but only on the most mundane and broadest of topics. "How are you today, Catlin?" "Fine. And what's the thrust of your speech today, Mr. Carr?"

She drove to his home in late October, to cover a special news conference. But seeing the house, softened and surrounded by the palette of autumn, left bittersweet memories throbbing and aching inside her mind and heart.

That house had seen hundreds of autumns. It had hosted the dreams of many generations. She left, without ever going to the conference; and told the station personnel that she had had car trouble. That night, on the competition's news, WTSB was scooped. Matthew Carr had announced that a spy from the Cleaver camp had been caught red-handed, stealing information from locked Carr campaign files. Naturally, Cleaver had denied any foreknowledge of the caper. But the information sent mild shock waves throughout the news community.

"Too bad," Maggie commented, entering Catlin's office the next afternoon. "I know how closely you've followed this one. And it's a darn shame you didn't get the story first."

Catlin shrugged. She had no one to blame but herself. Taylor had asked her to cover the conference, and she had let her own tattered emotions get in the way. She was slipping.

Maggie pulled up a chair and Catlin could tell that the woman wanted to talk. "What's up?" she asked, giving her an opening.

"Went to a luncheon today," Maggie began cautiously. "You know . . . that professional group of women in the news media I belong to."

Catlin nodded, giving Maggie plenty of time to gather her thoughts. "For some reason, Natalie Hartford was there," Maggie said and wrinkled her nose in distaste. "I can't begin to say how she can call herself a professional. Anyway, I talked to her." Maggie chose her words carefully. "She's been covering the social scene in this town for twenty years, you know."

Catlin leaned slightly forward as Maggie spoke.

"I asked her about Sandra Carr. Natalie covered everything the Van Cleefs did in her columns. In her opinion, Sandra was the darling of the circuit, if you get my drift."

"I do. What is it you're trying to tell me, Maggie?"

Maggie sighed heavily. "Now, boss, you know what a gossip that woman is. . . ."

149

"I know." Catlin sensed Maggie's distress. Her own mouth felt dry and she realized that she was holding her breath, hanging onto Maggie's words, both anticipating and dreading what she was about to hear.

"She said that Sandra's death wasn't exactly an accident." Maggie's quiet voice was more like a raspy whisper.

"What 'exactly' was it?" Catlin clenched her fists in her lap to stop her hands from shaking.

"Natalie said that what Sandra did—hitting the wall with her car—was done with 'malice afore-thought.' Sandra Carr did it on purpose. She killed herself."

CHAPTER 10

SUICIDE. THE VERY WORD was grotesque and dark. The ultimate act of anger. The final act of rejection. *Suicide.* The word, the ugliness of it, left Catlin cold and shaken.

"I–I hated to have to tell you," Maggie ventured. "But I knew you'd want to know."

Catlin nodded. Her mouth felt tight, but she forced the corners up in a smile of understanding and appreciation. "It's all right, Maggie. Thank you for digging it up."

Maggie asked, "Want me to pursue it any more?"

"No . . ." Catlin said. "No . . . I'll take it from here."

Maggie rose and went to the door of Catlin's office. "Hard to believe anyone could do that. Especially when it seemed she had everything in the world to live for. I wonder why she did it."

Why, indeed? Catlin sat alone, staring into space, a coldness clutching her body. What could have driven Sandra, the darling of society, the wealthy, pampered wife of Matthew Carr, to such an act? The black abyss

151

of Sandra's despair gaped in Catlin's consciousness—
a pit, a bottomless hole, a well of horror she couldn't
comprehend.

Who could give her the answers? Who could make
sense out of the grim reality of Sandra's act? Who
could banish the revulsion, the helplessness she felt?
Catlin knew there was only one answer to that
question. Only one source of the truth. And she had
access to that source. Slowly, she picked up her
phone and dialed Matthew Carr's private number.

He owed her nothing. She realized that as she drove
to his home in the cold darkness of the night. On the
phone, she had pled, "I have to see you, Matthew.
Please."

His voice sounded guarded, wary and distant. But
he had agreed to see her. That was something. The
guard admitted her to the estate property, and Matthew himself met her at the door of the silent, hollow
house and led her into the intimate warmth of his
study. He listened as she haltingly told him what she
had heard. His solemn green dappled eyes never left
her face.

"You have no reason to tell me," she said. "I know
that. No reason to give me any information. You said
once that this topic is off limits." She paused and met
his gaze directly, with unwavering appeal. "But for
what it's worth, you have my word that what you tell
me will never reach the media. You have my promise
as a journalist and . . ." she dropped her eyes, "and
as a friend."

He clasped his hands behind his head and stared up
at the ceiling for a long time. At last he turned to her
and asked, "Then why do you want to know,
Catlin?"

It was difficult to answer him. She wasn't sure
herself. Taylor had assigned Matthew to her as a
project, with specific instructions to "dig up something on him." At first, she had followed the directive.

152

But slowly, somewhere along the way—*where?* she wondered—she stopped seeing Matthew as an opportunist or an idealist or even as a politician. She saw him as a man. As a Christian.

She began to believe in what he represented. She began to care about him. So, now she answered him as best she could, from the depths of her confused feelings for him. "Because I just have to know. *I* have to know . . ." she added for emphasis.

His gaze traveled, unwavering, over her face, weighing, assessing. "It's a long story. And it starts long before I even entered Sandra's life."

Catlin nodded, trying hard to control the wild beating of her heart and the trembling of her hands. "I have all night," she told him.

"All right, Catlin," Matthew said quietly. "I'll tell you."

It took two hours. Two long, soul-wrenching hours. But, in the end, Catlin Burke felt she understood Sandra and the demons that had driven her. She also knew that Matthew had shared something with her that he had never shared with another human being. She ached for him, yet she listened with each of her senses tingling and taut.

Almost numb with fatigue, she whispered a trembling, "Thank you." Her mind reeled under the weight of the knowledge he had entrusted to her. "I–I need to be alone now," she told him candidly. "But may I call you back in a few days?" Her voice trembled slightly.

He agreed and she followed him to the door and left quickly. The cold, biting air revived her and cleared her head. She sorted and compartmentalized the information in her mind during the drive back to the station, putting the events into sequence, fitting the pieces together as in a jigsaw puzzle.

The night security man was surprised to see Catlin Burke at the entrance of the station so late at night.

He let her pass and she slipped down the darkened quiet halls to her office, where she gathered together all her files on Matthew Carr and reviewed and compiled the data she had gathered since the previous April.

Then she stripped the cover off her typewriter and wrote for two more hours. The words fell like sprinkled pepper onto the paper in her machine. Words that she knew no one would ever see, yet words that must be set down.

In the end, she felt that it was the best story she had ever written. More importantly, she knew she had presented the truth.

Sandra Newton Van Cleef was one of the American aristocracy. Although there were no titles in her lineage, no Counts, Dukes, or Lords, she held the esteemed distinction of belonging to one of the first families to settle in New England. It was an historical fact. Her forefathers had come as religious refugees from England. The Newtons blazed trails in the wilds of America, settled the best land along the Charles River, established a trading post at Boston Harbor and planted roots, deep and enduring. They emerged as pillars of the community—a cornerstone of the economic and social structure of the area.

The Van Cleefs married into the Newton family tree at the turn of the century when waves of European immigrants fled to the golden shores of America. Their new blood rejuvenated the solid Newton line, giving it an economic perspective it had previously lacked. The Van Cleef patriarch had a Midas touch. He turned moneymaking into an art form and built a financial empire that influenced American business for years to come.

The Van Cleefs ruled their interests with an air of removed ruthlessness. They were powerful. They were wealthy. And they survived when others failed in the Great Depression. The Van Cleefs set the tone for parties and balls and social and political causes. They wintered in Palm Beach. They spent their summers in Martha's Vineyard, overlooking Nantucket Bay. They returned to the secluded comfort of the famous family mansion perched serenely in the hills.

The great house still stands on vast green lawns, rambling and Victorian, looming monumental and stately, overlooking the woods and river originally walked off by Eustis Newton when he first established his homestead. Many architects had changed its face . . . added to its size and complexity, its great rooms, its balconies and porches, its splendid and unique motifs. It survived the Civil War and the political and economic wars of America's industrial age.

And the Van Cleefs survived with it. Cultured, unemotional people; generations of blond, blue-eyed, impeccably mannered people, well-educated, but aloof; and keeping their distance from the masses.

Sandra was the last of them. The only surviving child of Charles and Grace Van Cleef. The only child of an only child of an only child. Her mother had miscarried a stillborn son in her seventh month. Sandra was all that was left. Materially, she lacked for nothing. She had the finest that money could buy. And Van Cleef money bought a lot.

Charles was one of the last of a vanishing breed of economic patriarchs. One of the last power mongers who controlled and dominated his companies alone, unassisted by power-stripping mergers and committee-run corporations. His grandfather had forged deals with the Rockefellers, the Morgans, the Whitneys. The Van Cleefs survived when hundreds of their kind—fine families, rich in American heritage—did not.

Sandra was not without respect for her family's position and status. It was just that she found being a Van Cleef all very boring. Hers was a simmering nature, violent and churning beneath the quiet façade of the Van Cleef legacy. And it wasn't that her parents didn't love her. They just never quite knew what to do with her.

Sandra lived on an emotional pendulum that swung between wild bouts of ecstatic joy and uncontrolled activity to deep and dark depressions and sullen withdrawals. She lived on a seesaw, always teetering on the edge of some vast, lonely pit.

She first met Matthew Carr at a Greek mix on their college campus. He was already a campus hero, having led the football team to its first winning season in five years. He was everything she had ever found attractive in a man. Handsome, commanding, adored, and in firm control of himself, his world and his destiny.

They were attracted to each another immediately. Attracted in a primitive way, drawn by two separate and distinctive lifestyles. He had nothing: no name, no social prestige, no money. She had everything. And because she instinctively knew he wanted all the things she had, all the things denied him by his position of birth, she used them to get him.

That very night, she went back to her sorority house, called her fiancé, and broke their engagement. It was a clean, quick break. Simple. Neat. The announcement hadn't made the papers yet anyway. It made no difference that she had shattered the dreams of another man. She wanted the way clear for Matthew Carr.

Their courtship was stormy, often violent and scandalous. It became the topic of campus gossip. "Did you hear what Sandra and Matthew did last night?" They were an item. A thing. An event.

Her parents weren't overly impressed with her choice. At least not at first. They would have preferred that she marry one of her own kind— blueblooded, good social connections, very rich. But neither could find any true faults with Matthew. In fact, Charles began to develop a real fondness for the young man, recognizing in him a brilliant business sense, a shrewd inbred nature to make quick and calculated decisions, a natural ability to turn a little money into a lot of money.

Theirs was the quintessential wedding. The Van Cleefs opened their coffers and showered Sandra with everything she felt she needed to make all her girlhood dreams come true. The social columns had a field day, touting the wedding as the social event of the year. An invitation meant instant social prestige. Sandra considered it the high point of her life—the ultimate conquest. She had gotten Matthew, the one she had wanted from the first day she set eyes on him. Matthew considered it a circus.

But after the Van Cleef-Carrs settled into life at the family mansion—naturally Grace had had an extension built onto the back of the old mansion for the newlyweds—disillusionment settled over all of them. The elder Van Cleefs had looked upon Sandra's marriage to Matthew as a panacea, hoping he was capable of controlling and channeling their daughter's unbridled energies. Matthew had neither time nor interest in coddling his wife's erratic behavior nor in bowing to her manipulative ways.

Sandra never deluded herself that Matthew actually loved her. At least not in the romantic sense. For her, it became a constant battle to win him fully . . . for Matthew had a mistress—her father's business. It consumed him. And since he became, at least in spirit, the son Charles had always wanted, her father nurtured the affair, groomed the lover, and helped steal him away from his wife forever.

Sandra sought methods to regain Matthew's favor. Flamboyant, attention-seeking, destructive methods. She drank too much. She took too many pills, she drove too fast and got arrested once too often. Her

157

unpredictable and violent moods kept the family edgy and fearful. Matthew withdrew. He retreated into his work, into the demanding and challenging realm of business and moneymaking. He treated her changing moods with disgust and contempt. It only drove her to try harder.

At the age of seventy-five, Charles Van Cleef suffered a stroke. He died three months later after leaving everything to Matthew, with one stipulation. The fortune, the power—all of it was his—provided he remained with Sandra. Sandra's mother inherited Life Estate, but she died one year later, to the day.

Matthew, the heir apparent, took over full management and control of the Van Cleef empire. Matthew's days took on new vision and purpose. At thirty-one he was one of the wealthiest and most influential businessmen in the country. He wielded power on Wall Street. He set policy within his industry.

Both he and Sandra wanted children, and tried for the seven years of their marriage. Finally, after much frustration and testing, the doctors told her that she had a problem. Her Fallopian tubes were deformed, crimped. She could never conceive. Matthew tried to comfort and console her, but Sandra's moods became blacker, her depression obsessive. She stood at the edge of a darkening chasm, whose mouth yawned ever wider.

The simplest of tasks. Reproduction. A woman's inheritance. And Sandra Newton Van Cleef Carr— the girl who had everything—could not have a baby. She mixed her pills and her drinks one night. After a violent argument with Matthew, she left the mansion in a rage, and raced her sports car along the winding back roads without purpose, without destination.

The stone wall at the end of Walker Road had been there for sixty years. Everybody knew it. It was clearly marked. Either Sandra was too preoccupied to notice it on that evening, or she simply didn't care.

The police found some skid marks, as if her brakes had locked. But in the end, Sandra Carr hit the wall at sixty miles per hour.

Catlin read the story through twice. Then she covered her typewriter, gathered up all her files and documents on Matthew, slipped them into a larger portfolio and left the station. She drove through the cold, darkened streets and arriving at her apartment complex, parked and entered the warm, dim lobby. A security guard acknowledged her and she took the elevator up to her apartment and let herself in. The rooms felt cold. She shivered involuntarily.

Catlin quickly started a fire in the fireplace and stood watching the flames dance and crackle, holding out her hands to their warmth. Feeling suddenly exhausted, she showered beneath pelting hot fingers of water, then wrapped her slim body in a terrycloth robe and sat on her sofa, facing the fire.

She retrieved the portfolio and glanced at her clock. It was 3:00 A.M. Catlin opened the file folder and removed the neatly typed pages of her story. She read it through one last time. Then she rose, took the files and her story to the fireplace and carefully, page by page, dropped them into the dancing yellow flames.

She watched as the fire did its work, reducing the contents of each vanilla-colored file to ashes. She watched for a long time, staring into the mouth of the fireplace as the fire burned lower and lower. She watched until long after the flames died and the ashes had grown cold and gray.

"I want to know all of it, Matthew."

Catlin kept pace with his long strides through the woods behind the estate. The final glory of autumn hung on the trees overhead, and their shoes crunched across the blanket of leaves covering the floor of the woods.

"All of it?" he asked, glancing down at her. The brisk afternoon air nipped at them and swirled the leaves in pools and eddies at their feet.

"What you felt. . ." she explained. "How you coped. . . ."

Once again she had called and asked to see him. Once again he had set aside his schedule and welcomed her into his life. She had arrived at the mansion and they had eaten a light lunch together, in front of the ancient stone fireplace in the kitchen.

She felt awkward at first, but as they had sat and talked, her discomfort in his presence diminished. He treated her with an easy grace that helped her over the strained moments. The moments when she remembered their many partings.

After lunch, they bundled up in heavy, cable-knit sweaters. Catlin had slipped on a suede jacket also, and they walked outdoors, over the dying grass of the cultivated lawn and into the tangle of woods and trees that covered the back acres of the grounds.

He took her hand and she didn't draw away. "You mean after Sandra died, don't you?"

Catlin nodded.

"The guilt almost destroyed me," he said with complete candor. "You see, I was always a man in control of my own destiny. I had money, power, position. I spoke and things happened. But I had no control over Sandra. I couldn't love her enough. I couldn't give her enough of myself.

"And you see, I never really knew for sure if she meant to kill herself. Yet, somehow, I felt responsible." He stopped talking and they walked along in silence, while the leaves shuffled beneath their steps.

"I worked like a maniac. Trying to forget. Trying to fill up my life. Nothing worked for me. I couldn't forget."

She was surprised. "What turned you around?"

"I met Neal again. I was walking down the street

160

one spring afternoon and literally bumped into him. He had been my best friend once. Over the years we'd lost touch. Then one day, there he was again."

Catlin smiled. "And he invited you to church?" she asked, filling in the story in a gentle, teasing way.

Matthew laughed. "Not quite," he confessed. "I'm afraid I wouldn't have walked into any church just then. But he did invite me to a Christian business-men's breakfast. I thought Neal was nuts. But I went. For old time's sake.

"The place was filled with businessmen—wheeler-dealers, prominent, successful men. All like me. They had everything the world had to offer. Except, they seemed content and . . ." he searched for a word, "peaceful.

"There was a guest speaker at that breakfast. An evangelist. But not like any I'd ever seen before. He was articulate, educated, dynamic . . . on fire for God. I listened to him talk for an hour. And I knew that I wanted what that man had.

"Afterward, Neal brought him up here." Matthew gestured in the direction of the house. "We talked for hours. He helped me see that I wasn't responsible for Sandra's death . . . no more than I'd been responsible for her life. Like me, she alone was accountable for her own actions.

"I wanted the Kingdom of God, Catlin. I really wanted it. That was the turning point for me. I was saved and through Neal, found that church I took you to."

She remembered the church. And the peace and comfort she had experienced there.

His voice was resonant, weaving a spell of intensi-ty. "The minister taught me, shepherded me, disci-pled me. I met May and Dodd. I've spent four years getting ready for God's purposes. When the doors opened to run for State Senator. . ." he shrugged. Halting suddenly on the path, he turned her to face him. "The rest, as they say, is history."

She looked long and deep into his eyes and her heart swelled with renewed feeling for him. An errant autumn leaf fluttered down and caught in her hair. He reached to remove it and the touch of his fingers caused an involuntary shiver to travel down her spine.

He drew her hands to his lips and encountered the hardness of her ring. He looked at the beautiful stone for a long moment. "I see you're still engaged." It was a comment, not a question. "Do you love Taylor Shentell?" His question was open and inquiring. Not malicious or prying. She pulled her hands away and sighed.

"I–it's complicated. . . ."

"How complicated can love be, Catlin?"

She stepped away from him and resumed walking. He was by her side at once, matching her, stride for stride. How could she explain it to him? How could she feel what she did for him and still be pledged to another man?

They walked through the dead, dry leaves, bending under low, bare tree branches. The sky turned a leaden gray and the wind increased, sounding mournful in the woods surrounding them.

"Are you . . . is the bullet wound . . ." She struggled to change the subject.

"It's a good thing I don't have to throw a football for a living," he half-joked. "The scar is right near the joint of my shoulder. I'm not as flexible as I used to be."

"But it is healed?" Her tone sounded anxious.

"*That* wound is healed . . ." he added cryptically. Then he stopped, took her by her shoulders and looked down at her from his full height.

She felt the old familiar longing for him rising up again. The old forbidden longing. . . .

The gray sky above framed his head and the breeze caused his hair to fall across his forehead in windswept layers. He tenderly traced his forefinger along the arch of her cheekbone. "And now I think we'd better go back to the house and you'd better leave," he said, his voice husky and compelling. "Because if you don't leave soon, I'm going to kiss you. And if I kiss you, I won't let you leave."

They walked back, briskly, without speaking. She felt strangely close to him—close and somehow linked by some invisible thread. He was right, of course. The physical attraction between them was dangerous. Dangerous and explosive. She couldn't trust herself to be too long alone with him.

I'm engaged! She told herself fiercely over and over during the drive back to her apartment. *I'm going to marry Taylor. It's all set.* But as she whipped into her parking space at her apartment complex, she struck the steering wheel with a clenched fist and with such force that she bruised the side of her hand.

"You seem distracted tonight, Cat." The comment came from Taylor as he reached across the restaurant table and took her hand in his.

Catlin pulled away slightly and resumed her task of pushing food around her plate with the prongs of her fork. "Sorry . . ." she told him. "I guess I'm just tired. . . ."

Taylor leaned against his chair and appraised her. She squirmed beneath his probing stare and let her eyes wander over the intimate groupings of tables and diners in the elegant eatery. Their special, reserved table was situated next to the glass wall that overlooked the city of Boston. Hundreds of feet below, the twinkling lights of the city flickered and danced.

From this vantage point, it appeared as if some giant hand had sprinkled sequins randomly over the city, and stretched long ribbons of light across the hills in the distance. Yet she couldn't appreciate its beauty. There were too many conflicting emotions raging within.

"The show is selling nicely," Taylor ventured, as if that carrot would prick her interest and drag her out of her introspective mood. "We'll go into production in January," he added when she didn't respond. "Once the election and the wedding are out of the way. . . ."

She laid her fork down and eyed him thoughtfully. "You know, Taylor," she began, "in two months we'll be married, and I don't think we've ever once talked about anything concerning married life."

He cocked his head. "Is that what's eating you?" he asked, a bit annoyed. "Pre-wedding jitters?"

She ignored his comment. "What are our goals after we're married? Do you want children, Taylor? Where will we live? For that matter, will we be married in a church or by a justice of the peace?" Her tone had grown sarcastic, but she didn't try to disguise it.

"Good grief, Cat . . ." his voice took on an edge of annoyance. "Of course, we'll be married in a church. Pick any one you want and I'll arrange it. I'll build you the biggest house in Boston . . . or, if you want, we can renovate one of those places on Beacon Street. We can live in my condo until you decide. As for children . . . I don't care. I grew up in a big family, and it doesn't matter to me one way or another." He paused. "Although, I will say I'm not crazy about sharing you with a houseful of kids. . . ."

Catlin took a long sip from her water goblet and set it down hard. It sloshed onto the white linen tablecloth and Taylor let out an exasperated breath. "If kids are important to you, then we'll have them!" he placated.

"Children are *not* the issue!" she snapped. "*We* are the issue. Taylor, what do we have in common except WTSB and the TV show you're preparing?" He looked stricken and she half-regretted her sharp words.

"I love you," he said earnestly. "I want you to be mine. Totally and completely mine. Why isn't that enough?"

"Because it just isn't . . ." she said, her voice pleading, her eyes appealing. "I–I feel so . . . so . . . stifled!"

"Not by me," he denied. "I want to give you the world, Catlin—everything I have, all I've worked for all my life. I want to share it with you." He reached over and this time caught her hand and refused to release it. "I won't let you go. Not ever." His eyes blazed with intensity and she dropped her own gaze, conscious of the stares of others.

"I'll be glad when the election's over . . ." she said and then wondered at such an inane, off-the-topic comment.

"So will I," Taylor said. And he raised her captive hand to his lips and kissed it possessively.

As November descended on the state, the final frenzied days of the campaign filled the media, the news, conversations of people everywhere. Already, some pollsters had said the outcome was "too close to call." Catlin didn't doubt it.

She kept to the fringes of Matthew's political life and reported dutifully to her evening viewers about the impending election. She kept her reports impersonal, fact-filled and honest. She gave Cleaver and Nolan equal time and wished for the whole process to be over as quickly as possible.

Matthew appeared on network telecasts each evening, and Catlin watched with keen interest. They called him "The Golden Man of Politics." He had virtually accomplished the impossible, rising from a political nobody to a political presence in two years. His platform of Christian values had endeared him to the people, not alienated them per earlier predictions. The entire country was watching the outcome of the Massachusetts Senatorial election.

As she watched his image center on the TV monitor screens of WTSB daily, and heard what the great network commentators had to say about him, she recalled again and again the feel of his mouth, the touch of his hands. In a few days it would be over. Matthew would either win or lose, but he would be out of her life, once and for all. She both desired and dreaded that inevitability.

In the meantime she busied herself with other stories, struggling to get back in the groove of investigative reporting. She scoured the city for potential stories, dragging Red along on numerous false leads. *Busy* . . . she told herself. *I have to stay busy.* Work acted as a balm for her battered emotions.

The Friday morning before the Tuesday election, she returned to a pile of pink message slips on her desk. She scanned them quickly, half hoping that one of them was from Matthew. Instead, there were two from Leo Kelly. Her curiosity piqued.

She reached for her phone and dialed his number at the newspaper. "Now what can Leo possibly want?" she mused aloud.

CHAPTER 11

As it turned out, Leo wanted to meet her for lunch. She joined him in a small pub near Harvard Square, smoke-filled and pungent with the smell of sausage and beer. Heads turned as she entered from the cold blast of the streets and slipped into the cushioned booth in the back next to Leo. He toasted her with his beer mug.

"Such a picture!" He beamed her a genuine smile. "Let them eat their hearts out!" he added, with a wave of his beefy fingers to the room of admiring males.

She smiled impishly and fell into the camaraderie of his mood. "I thought you had no use for television newspersons."

"You are different, Miss Burke." For the first time, she detected a bit of an Irish brogue in his voice.

"And to what do I owe the honor of this summons?"

His answer was interrupted by the arrival of a waiter. "Coffee for the lady," Leo told him, "and a big bowl of Irish stew." He peered over at her and she nodded her approval of his menu selection.

"It grieves me," Leo began once the waiter had left, "that I have been spending so much time alone on Mr. Carr's campaign. Where have you been hiding yourself?"

She shrugged noncommittally. "Taylor Shentell thought WTSB had spent enough time and energy on Carr's campaign. . . ."

"Too bad . . ." Leo told her. "That bus has been a dark and lonely place without your sunshine, Miss Burke."

"Why, Mr. Kelly!" she gasped in mock humility. "You'll turn my head with your Irish tongue." He guffawed and took a swig from his mug. "Now just why did you invite me to lunch?"

"Professional courtesy." He reached inside his sports jacket and pulled out several folded sheets of paper. "It's my next column," he explained. "It's going into Sunday's issue of the Globe. My unqualified endorsement of Matthew Carr."

Her eyes widened as she took the papers and scanned the neat type. Leo Kelly was backing Matthew unconditionally! Her heart leaped. That meant hundreds of dailies all over the state would follow suit.

She gave him a beautiful smile. "That's wonderful, Leo! Thank you for telling me. You think he's going to win, don't you?"

"If all those Christians get off their duffs and go to the polls Tuesday," he affirmed. "But voters are a fickle lot. A little bad weather, . . ." he snapped his fingers, "and 'poof'! They vanish."

"You believe in him, don't you Leo?"

"I believe he'll be a good thing for this state. And ultimately, a good thing for this country. But he wears his Christianity a little too blatantly on his sleeve for my taste. At least he's got principles. That's more than I can say for most of them."

Catlin tasted the piping-hot stew the waiter set

168

before her and felt its warmth heighten her already bouyant spirits. Leo Kelly was endorsing Matthew! It would make a difference in his chances. She knew it would!

"What's Shentell going to do?" he asked, probing but cautious.

Catlin shrugged. "Nothing. It's not station policy to endorse candidates. I mean, he never has before. Why do you ask?"

Leo eyed her. "I just wondered." He rolled his words slowly. "What with the bad blood between them. . . ."

Catlin arched her eyebrow, truly surprised by Leo's offhanded revelation. "Bad blood?" She had had no knowledge of problems between Taylor and Matthew, only a vague uneasiness that she could not define.

"I'm not talking out of school," Leo defended quickly. "But several years back, Taylor used that Ken Anderson fellow to take regular swipes at Carr on the air. Hounded him, in fact. It was before you came . . . so I guess they must have worked out their differences. . . ."

Catlin's surprise mingled with anger. She had suspected that Taylor had never liked Matthew, but he'd never hinted at the reasons. "I really don't know anything about it." She tried to hide her inner turmoil by concentrating on the stew, but she had lost her appetite.

Just when all the pieces seemed to be fitting in the puzzle, something turned up to throw the entire picture out of focus. Catlin didn't like it. Not one bit! She decided to say nothing more to Leo, but she would certainly ask Taylor about it at the first opportunity.

They finished their lunch amid a flow of light banter, and if Leo sensed her ire over his revelation, he didn't mention it. Following lunch, she thanked him again for allowing her to preview his upcoming column, then went straight to WTSB.

Back at the station, she discovered that Taylor had left on an unexpected business trip, with a scribbled note that he would see her on Monday morning. The delay frustrated her. Her query would have to wait. She couldn't ask Matthew. Not now. Not with a full schedule of last-minute campaigning. No . . . she would wait and talk to Taylor. After all, she was working for him. He owed it to her.

She spent the weekend alone. She read. She cooked. She worked on a piece of needlepoint. She kept herself busy. Rote tasks occupied her mind. Kept her thoughts from churning and from idle speculation. She decided to confront Taylor first thing Monday morning. Taylor was a creature of habit. By nine in the morning, he would be alone in his office, reading his mail and formulating his agenda. He often sent for her then, during those quiet morning hours. She would see him and ask her questions. All her questions.

The Monday morning summons to his office brought Catlin quickly, but her agitation and questions died on her lips when she saw him. Taylor Shentell was in a rage. She found him pacing in his office like a caged animal.

"Curse that Leo Kelly!" Taylor spat when she entered. "Why would he do this?" Taylor slung the folded newspaper section across his office and glared at Catlin.

"Do what?" she gasped, stunned by his hostility.

"Endorse Carr! What else?"

"Now, wait a minute. . . ." Catlin advanced toward him. "It's still a free country. Leo Kelly can endorse whomever he chooses. . . ."

"Do you know what kind of weight that man pulls with the voters?" Taylor fumed.

"A lot of weight."

"Then, this just might be the element that sends Carr over the top." Taylor paused and looked out into

170

the garden outside his glass wall. The tree was now bare, and the weak morning sun emphasized the stark, dead look.

Catlin suppressed a shiver. "Why does that bother you so, Taylor?"

He ignored her. "Well I know what to do to counter Kelly's action," Taylor slammed his fist into his open palm. "In fact, I've already set the wheels in motion."

"What are you talking about?" she asked, confused and bewildered by his irrationality.

"WTSB is going to endorse Cleaver!" he told her triumphantly. "Tonight, on the 'Six o'clock News', the eve of the election. We're going on the air with a special editorial backing Cleaver. And you're going to present it." His eyes glittered with anticipation.

Catlin felt the color drain from her face. She stood, staring at him, her mouth agape, her mind numb. Finally she managed to gasp, "What are you saying?"

"I said, WTSB is going to endorse Cleaver tonight on the news. I'll write the editorial myself. I'll tell engineering to start setting up Studio A. You can pretape it this afternoon and we'll log it into tonight's telecast. That way, we can rerun it at eleven o'clock, too." His voice snapped with excitement as he reached for his phone.

Catlin's mind reeled and her feet felt planted and wooden. "No," she said softly.

Taylor stopped abruptly and raised his eyes to meet hers. "What?"

Catlin stepped forward and leaned closer to him. "I said no. I won't do that editorial."

Taylor stared at her in open-mouthed disbelief. "I beg your pardon?"

She spoke firmly, her words considered and deliberate. "I will not read such an editorial, Taylor. It would make no sense."

"I still set policy at this station, Catlin," Taylor

reminded her darkly. "You work for me. Keep your personal feelings to yourself. You do what you want in the voter's booth tomorrow. But tonight, on my station, you'll give an editorial endorsing Cleaver."

She crossed her arms and rocked back on her heels. "For months I've faithfully followed Carr's campaign. I've brought report after report to my viewers about his integrity, his Christian platform, his sincerity. . . . Report after report. Good reports." She kept her voice low, firm and steely. "My public believes me. And now, you want me to go on the air and throw all that away? I won't do it."

Taylor snorted in disgust. "Your reputation as a journalist!" He slung the words at her. "I made your reputation in this market," he said hotly. "I created you!"

Her temper flared. "You gave me my break, Taylor. But *I* made my reputation. And I won't go on the record endorsing a man like Cleaver over Matthew Carr."

He glared at her, took a deep breath, and his voice took on a conciliatory tone. "Look . . . I met with Cleaver this weekend. The guy's served this state for three terms. He's got seniority in Washington. He has the ear of other senators. All this corruption talk . . . well, it can't be proved. I don't believe it's true."

Catlin grew incredulous. "You met with him? Actually met and discussed endorsing him?"

His face reddened. "I know what I'm doing!"

"Why, Taylor?" Catlin probed, her voice growing low and demanding. She glared at him through narrowed golden eyes. "Why do you hate Carr so much?"

He ignored her question. "I've got an editorial to write," he said briskly, shuffling papers on his desk. "Now, if you have some pertinent input, I'll be glad to consider it."

"Write it!" Catlin shouted. "But get someone else

to deliver it. Because I won't!'' She spun on her heels and flew to the door of his office, jerking it open with a vengeance.

"Stop!" Taylor bounded after her. They were in the hallway and their fight became public knowledge. Heads peered from various office doors. Mouths gaped in open amazement. Catlin ignored them.

She swept down the hall with heated determination. Taylor did not follow, but he called after her, "Cool off, Miss Burke. We'll be taping in two hours. For your sake, you'd better be here!"

She didn't bother to answer his veiled threat. She went directly to her office, grabbed her coat and purse, and left WTSB as quickly as she could.

Catlin returned to her apartment, her anger cresting in waves of physical sensation. She paced and trembled and simmered in her ocean of anger and wrath. Why? Why? The question haunted her. It taunted and teased at her subconscious. It wrapped around her spirit in snake-like tendrils. Why?

The realization that she had walked out on her job, her assignments, her commitments also lay heavy on her. In all her working years, she had never missed a deadline, never let down her co-workers, never failed to go on the air when expected. Night after night, month after month, for four years, she'd delivered the news telecast from the WTSB studio. Except tonight. . . .

The jangle of her telephone caused her to start. She reached for it, paused, glanced at her clock. It was exactly 11:00 A.M. She withdrew her hand, ignoring the instrument's raucous demands. The issue was settled. The station was beginning to tape the editorial, and she would not be the one to deliver its message.

Ken. Of course. Taylor would get Ken Anderson to read it. "That will certainly make your day, won't it, Ken?" she asked into the vacant air of her living room. She was positive that Ken would also be responsible for delivering the six o'clock newscast. It would be "business as usual" at the station. Her mouth twisted in an ironic smile. Would she be missed? Would the viewers defend her? What had her stand cost her?

Matthew . . . The thought of him came floating into her thoughts like a leaf on a summer pond. He would miss her. And he would be hurt the most by the WTSB editorial. "I have to tell him . . ."

Catlin made several calls, but could not track him down. An urgency nipped at her. She wanted him to know—before the newscast was delivered. And she wanted him to know that she had had no part in its treachery.

She ended up calling May Brighton. The woman's gentle hello gave Catlin an odd sense of serenity. Quickly Catlin told May about the editorial.

"I–I couldn't reach Matthew," she finished into the receiver. "Please, May . . . get the message to him somehow."

"I will," May assured her. "Thank you, Catlin. I'm very glad you told us."

"I had nothing to do with Taylor's decision . . ."

"I know that. . . . Are you all right?" May's tender inquiry made a lump rise in Catlin's throat. It was so typical of her to be concerned for someone else.

"I'm fine. I–I just have a lot of thinking to do. A lot of sorting out."

"If you need anything. . . ."

"Thank you," Catlin whispered.

"I'll be praying for you," May said.

Catlin's voice caught in her throat. She hung up and then unplugged her phone. Finally she sat down to wait. She waited for the minutes to tick away. For time to pass. For the hands of the clock to finish their journey to six P.M.

At six o'clock, she switched on her television set.

174

The WTSB news set looked like it always did—with one notable exception. Ken Anderson promoed the headlines, introduced the weather and sports anchors, and delivered the evening news. Her name was mentioned only once, to inform viewers that "Catlin Burke is on assignment." It was a lie, but at least there would be no switchboard inquiries.

Grimly she sat and watched Ken deliver her stories. She watched his smiling face, smooth delivery, and calm, assured manner. She heard him say the words she should be saying, to the camera, to the thousands of viewers who watched nightly. She almost regretted her actions. Then the editorial appeared.

Ken delivered a wholehearted endorsement of Cleaver and a subtle, snide attack on Matthew. Nothing libelous. Taylor Shentell was too clever for that. But the innuendo, the general derision in Ken's style left no doubt as to the management's sympathies. Her anger welled again, in fresh hot waves.

With one swift motion, she switched off the set and paced the room. Again the question, why? seeped into her mind, surfacing through the anger and confusion. Again it was like looking at a jigsaw puzzle. At first, all the pieces had seemed to drop into place—at least those regarding Sandra and Matthew. But something was still missing. The dead center of the puzzle.

A vision of Catlin's childhood friend Christine Harrold came drifting to the surface of her mind from out of nowhere. The corners of Catlin's mouth turned up. She thought of all the times she and Christine had put together puzzles on the dining room table of her parents' home. Hundreds of puzzles. Millions of pieces. Getting them through the summer doldrums. Christine always hid one piece—the last piece. It used to infuriate Catlin, but the girl had a fetish about putting in the last piece. Her excuse was usually the same: "It must have dropped under the table." But she always managed to be the one to insert that final piece. And until she did, the puzzle wasn't complete.

It was like that now. This puzzle wasn't complete. There was no Christine hiding pieces either. No . . . Catlin had simply overlooked something.

She closed her eyes and sank back against her sofa, visualizing the files she had burned. She recalled conversations with Taylor, Matthew, Maggie, Leo. She flipped through months of information. Through banks of compiled memories. The words she had written came into the pages of her mind. Crisp, clean black letters on fresh, white paper. The truth lay staring at her.

Catlin sat bolt upright. In one blinding flash, she knew the truth. Like sunlight pouring into a dark room, it all but blinded her. She caught her breath with the impact of the realization, flushed hot, then cold with the force of the revelation. In that one insightful moment, Catlin Burke knew why. *She knew!*

Catlin planned her arrival at the station with calculation. She waited until the evening crews had left for their dinner break, allowing herself plenty of time before they would return to set up the eleven o'clock news show. Taylor would be in his office alone.

The November night was frigid and biting, with a bone-chilling breeze from the North. But it wasn't the cold that affected her. The enormity of the confrontation with Taylor chilled her far more intensely than the night wind could penetrate her body.

She entered the artificial warmth of the station and walked purposefully down the silent executive halls of WTSB to the office at the end—Taylor's office. She entered without knocking. He sat behind his desk, his fingertips pressed together, his face a mask of brooding. He glanced up, surprised. He came to his feet quickly, started to cross over to her, a look of relief flooding his face. But he caught himself and waited, his features frozen.

176

"Welcome back, Catlin." His voice cracked, icy and sarcastic.

She ignored him and took a deep breath. "You were the man, weren't you, Taylor?"

A look of confusion swept his face, momentarily replacing the wall of anger. "What?"

She took a step toward him and said more boldly, "Before Sandra met and married Matthew, she was engaged to another man. *You* were that man, weren't you?"

His color drained. "That was a long time ago. . . ."

"Not long enough!" she said hotly. "Not so long that you've forgotten *or* forgiven!" Indignation filled her at his admission.

Suddenly, his face contorted and he placed his palms flat on his desk and leaned toward her threateningly. "She was *mine* . . ." he growled. "Imagine! Poor trash like me, social refuse . . . and I managed to attract the attention of Sandra Van Cleef. She would have married me. . . ." His voice dropped with the vividness of his memories. "Carr took her from me . . ."

Catlin reeled with the fury of his hate, the distortion of his logic. "I could have had it *all!*" Taylor fired. "All of it! Sandra, the Van Cleef empire, all of it!"

Her mouth dropped in amazement. "You got it *all* anyway . . ." she said, gesturing with a wave of her hand around the room.

His mouth twisted in a cruel smile. "Yes . . . I did, didn't I? But I wanted her, too. . . . She was mine. She promised me. . . ."

Catlin felt a shiver pass over her and her stomach constricted with revulsion. "She fell in love with another man, Taylor," she said quietly. "It happens."

Yet, deep down, Catlin knew that the situation had been much more complex. Sandra hadn't just "fallen in love with Matthew." She had sought him, coveted him, determined to have him. Her affair with Taylor had been a whim . . . a diversion . . . an amusement. And she had broken it off as casually as if she had clipped a hangnail.

"She regretted it, you know. . ." Taylor mused, staring off at some unseen vision. "She told me so. Years after they were married. She came to me and told me she was sorry she'd married him. That it had been a foolish mistake. I begged her to divorce him . . . but she wouldn't . . ." His voice fell to a hushed whisper.

Catlin almost saw the meetings as Taylor described them, perceiving Sandra's motives with insightful clarity. Visualizing the woman manipulating and using Taylor, struggling with focused vengeance to hurt and humiliate Matthew.

"He killed her." Taylor spat the accusation with venom. "Just as surely as if he'd driven that car himself, Matthew Carr killed her."

Incredulously, Catlin gaped at him. "Taylor, that's not true!" she gasped. "Sandra was a poor, sick, driven woman. A manic-depressive . . . hurt, resentful. . . . She made her own choices. She did her own driving."

His gaze flew to her face and he asked savagely, "How do you know?"

Stunned and fearful, Catlin stepped backward. She reined in her emotions and her fears with iron resolve. "I won't argue the past with you, Taylor. I wasn't there. But I was here the night you called me in and assigned me to Carr's campaign. You used me, Taylor. With cruelty and deliberation. You used me.

"I was supposed to 'find something on Carr' and 'expose him,' wasn't I? It didn't matter what it cost me. It didn't matter who was destroyed in the process. I was your weapon to stop Matthew."

Taylor blanched, but his eyes blazed. "No!" he shouted, coming around his desk. "Never! I love you, Cat!"

178

"Love me?" she asked sardonically. "You don't know the meaning of the word." She didn't wait for him to reach out for her. She stepped to his glass-topped round table. Although the drapes were pulled across the outside window, she felt the chill of the night through the folds. With swift deliberation, she removed the diamond from her finger and slammed it down on the tabletop. Its flawless facets cut a long, jagged mark on the glass surface . . . a scar, a wound. Taylor winced.

"No . . ." he choked. "I want you, Catlin! I love you . . . We'll start again. . . ."

"I'm sorry, Taylor. It's too late." She turned and crossed to the open door. She had to get out! Had to escape. Had to get far away from him, his presence, his avenging hatred and cloying possessiveness.

"Stop!" he shouted as she ran down the hallway to the freedom of the night. "Catlin, come back! I swear to you, if you leave, you'll never work in this business again! I'll see to it that no one hires you—ever!"

His words hit her like well-aimed stones, leaving behind an aching bruise. Her career . . . it was over. But she didn't stop. And she didn't look back. She ran to the front door, past a stunned nightwatchman, and out into the bitter cold night. Somehow she managed to get to her car, to turn the ignition key, to shove the automobile into gear. She clenched the steering wheel to still her wildly trembling hands before turning out of the parking lot.

The car catapulted forward as if shot from a sling. Catlin felt hot tears in her eyes and the lights of the streetlamps shimmered and danced through her veiled vision. It was over. All over. Everything she had worked for, fought for, lived for. Her life lay in ruins around her.

". . . Faith is letting go and trusting God to catch you. . . ." Matthew's words struggled up from the crevices of her mind, a rope in her mire of quicksand.

She was alone. Totally alone and she was scared. The darkness stretched before her in an unbroken ribbon.

And because she did not know what else to do, Catlin Burke prayed. . . .

CHAPTER 12

"CATLIN!"

The sound of Matthew's voice calling her name broke her tenuous hold on composure and she burst into sobs. She stood, shivering on the doorstep of the great mansion, while the bright light of the foyer chandelier surrounded him with an aura of light. When he reached for her protectively, she fell into his arms, burying her tear-streaked face in the warm haven of his shoulder.

He drew her inside, out of the chilling cold, out of the darkness, into the circle of warmth and light. He stroked her hair and whispered her name again and again, holding her to him until her violent sobbing had subsided and she clung, exhausted and drained in his embrace.

Finally he led her into the den, lowered her gently to the sofa, and sat beside her, stroking and soothing her. She relinquished her despair in increments, releasing first the tears, then the shuddering, and lastly, the grief.

When he was sure she could speak, he asked, "What happened? Please tell me what happened?"

"I–It all blew up tonight. . . ." Her voice was hoarse, halting. "Taylor . . . I–I left him . . . my job . . . everything. I didn't know where else to go. . . . So I came here. . . ." She turned her golden eyes toward him, and he took her face between his palms and stared into their depths.

"I'm glad you came to me. . ." he said softly. "I love you. . . ."

His words engulfed her and she leaned forward to receive his kiss, a gratitude and a sense of wonder pulsing through her heart. "Oh, Matthew!" she cried and flung her arms around his neck.

He held her fast, stroking her hair. When he pulled away, he said, "Tell me everything, Catlin. Tell me the whole story."

She struggled with the words at first, searching for them, speaking them carefully when she found them, but she told him all she knew. All that had happened to her over the past months. "He used me," she finished, drained, but no longer angry. "He wanted to wreck your campaign. And he tried to use me to do it."

Matthew said nothing. He watched her and she looked back at him for one long moment. New waves of revelation washed over her. She pushed back, momentarily stunned. "You knew!" she gasped. "You've known all along! About Taylor, Sandra, Taylor's hatred for you. . . ." Her cheeks flamed as a sense of renewed betrayal and distrust coursed through her.

She struggled to get up, but he caught her firmly and held her in a vise-like grip. "Yes," Matthew acknowledged, "I knew. But what was I supposed to do about it?" His quiet logic calmed her and she stopped struggling. "Would you have believed me if I'd told you? Would you have listened?" He shook his head, answering his own question. "It wasn't easy, Catlin. When you became engaged, I almost went crazy. The

182

thought of your actually marrying him. . . ." His voice dropped, his tone pained. "But you had to find out for yourself. And I had to trust God to handle it in His way. To reveal it to you in His timing. I never wanted you to be hurt."

He smiled, a half-smile, and his green-flecked eyes burned into her. "Shentell's always hated me. I thought he'd gotten over it. But instead, he turned bitter and hard. And bitterness is like an acid. It eats away from the inside out . . . pitting . . . destroying. Outwardly, he never changed. But inside. . . ." He let the implication of his words sink into her.

"Oh, Matthew," she murmured into his shoulder, "I'm so sorry." Privately, she wondered how Sandra could have influenced and corrupted so many lives. So many dreams. . . .

Catlin recoiled, unable to focus on the enormity of the tangled and intricate web of lies and hurt and pain the Van Cleef heir had left behind her. "I'm so tired. . . ." she confessed to Matthew, totally drained of emotion. "I don't know what to do right now. I can't face the thought of going back to my apartment. What if Taylor comes after me? . . ." She shivered and Matthew pulled her closer to him.

"Then stay here," he offered.

"That would make great reading in tomorrow's papers," she told him wearily.

"It's an honorable offer," he said, stroking her hair, twining the thick strands through his fingers. Her pulse quickened as his voice dropped husky and soft. "Believe me, pretty lady, you don't have to fear for your reputation, though I'll have to confess you're the biggest temptation that has come along." He paused. "Neal and Dodd are in the kitchen. We're writing speeches."

For the first time in hours, she remembered the campaign. The next morning was election day! Why, Matthew had the weight of the world on him now! "I–

I forgot! Oh, Matthew, how *could* I have forgotten?" She lifted her stricken face to his.

"We'll be up all night anyway," he explained. "I want the speeches to be ready for tomorrow night—whether acceptance or concession."

"You'll be elected!" she said with spirit. "Regardless of Taylor's editorial, I know you'll be elected!"

He chuckled and hugged her. "Nothing he said hurt me. Either I win tomorrow, or I lose. It's in God's hands." He stood and pulled her up beside him. Now, I'm taking you upstairs and tucking you in."

She protested. "But Matthew, I have nothing with me. Not even a toothbrush!"

"I have everything you need," he assured her. "May always keeps a guest room stocked and ready for company. We entertain for business purposes quite often. At least this old museum is good for privacy."

He circled her shoulders with his arm and took her into the hallway, through the foyer, and up the stairs. On the landing, she averted her eyes from the massive portrait that loomed down from the wall, and buried herself in Matthew's embrace. Still holding her close against his side, he hesitated before a pale yellow door on the second floor, turned the knob, and flicked on the switch.

"Matthew," she pulled back slightly to look up into his face. "There's something else I need to tell you." Catlin struggled to put her brimming emotions into words. "I know I said that I came here because I had no place else to go. That wasn't exactly true. I came here—to you—because I believe God wanted me to."

"Tell me."

"When I left the station, when I thought I was all alone and out of options—" her eyes grew soft as she relived her experience, "—I remembered what you'd told me once. About trusting God to catch you. I—I'd

184

never felt so isolated, so scared . . . and . . . and I asked Him to help me. Matthew, suddenly I felt His presence with me in the car. I felt His Spirit and—and I knew I wasn't alone anymore. I know that no matter what happens, I'll never be alone again."

Her voice had dropped to a whisper and she saw a smile flip the corners of Matthew's lips. His eyes burned bright and tender. His hand cupped her chin. "I'll be here for you too, Catlin. Tonight. Tomorrow. Always."

"You've been here for me all along. Even when I thought I didn't need you." Her love for him bubbled inside her like a wellspring. She was reluctant to let go of him, afraid that if she did, he might evaporate into the air. "I love you, Matthew. I love *who* you are. I love *what* you are."

He tipped back her chin with the crook of his finger. His eyes danced mischievously and his voice was low, provocative. "I know, Miss Burke. But it certainly took *you* long enough to figure it out."

She blushed crimson, and let him brush her lips with his. "Go to bed," he commanded gently. "You need some rest. We'll talk about it all tomorrow."

She slipped into the bedroom and closed the door quietly behind her. With her eyes closed, she leaned against the solid wood that had lasted for two centuries. Her heart pounded. It was true! She loved him. And he loved her. She felt warm, safe, enthralled by the magnitude of her discovery.

Renewed weariness overtook her as she looked around the room. It glowed with May's feminine, homey touches. The walls were papered in a rosy-floral print; the wainscoting and wood trim were painted ivory. A maple fourposter bed stood centered on an enormous braided rug, bordered by dark oak floorboards.

She ran her hand over a poster finial. Its hard, round shape felt solid. She smoothed the antique lace

185

bed spread and pulled it back to reveal inviting, fresh-smelling cotton sheets beneath a down comforter. The fragrance of rose water floated from the pillowcases, and she decided that she could not possibly crawl between such lovely sheets, fully clothed.

She explored a dresser along the wall and found a satin sleeping gown folded neatly in one drawer. She slipped into an adjoining bathroom, undressed, and pulled the silky gown over her shivering body. She washed her face with finely milled rose soap, luxuriating in the thick, white lather. She appraised herself in a full length dressing mirror . . . an old-fashioned kind framed in wood and free-standing, swiveling to her touch.

The ivory gown dropped smoothly from her shoulders, revealing the soft curves of her body. Her hair lay in full, soft auburn waves around her face and neck. She touched her arms and imagined Matthew holding her. "I love you, Matthew," she told her reflection, reveling in the sound of the words.

Catlin drifted into the bedroom, stood briefly at the window and listened to the scratching of tree branches in the inky, cold blackness. She was no longer afraid of the night. God had heard her prayer. He had caught her and delivered her, safe and protected, into Matthew's life. A loving gratitude filled her and replaced her restlessness with peace. Her prayer of thanks to the wonderful, loving God of her childhood was brief and awed.

She turned off the light and slid between the smooth, rose-scented sheets. She was exhausted, but her mind kept spinning. The old house creaked and groaned with the whispers of time. Her mind filled again with visions of grand balls, sumptuous parties . . . voices of the siren past. Calling . . . singing . . . whispering. The melody of wind . . . the softness of down pillows . . . the spreading warmth of her thick down quilt lulled Catlin into a sleep of forgetfulness.

Deep, quiet, healing sleep. A respite from the fury of the day's storm.

In her dreams, Catlin drifted through a summer meadow rippling with tall, green waves of wind-blown grass, redolent with the smell of wildflowers. She walked across the meadow in a satin dressing gown, aimless, pausing to touch the fragrant blossoms.

Far away in the distance, she saw a tree. And beyond the tree, a house. She felt an urgency, as if someone were waiting there for her. But she was apprehensive about passing under the tree. She hurried along, swerving in a wide path to avoid it. But no matter how hard she tried to circumvent the tree, it kept springing into her pathway, forcing her to pass beneath it.

The tree grew larger. She squared her shoulders and resolved to walk quickly, to get it behind her. But as she drew closer, she saw a huge painting swaying on hinged hooks. It was the portrait of a woman in a blue satin ball gown. Catlin gazed at it for a long moment, puzzled. The picture seemed so familiar. Why couldn't she place the image?

The portrait swung lower, blocking her way. Catlin tried to go around it, but it dropped lower still. Now she was growing frantic to reach the house. She reached out to push the painting aside. But it felt solid and immovable, like a stone wall.

A mild panic welled up within her. She shoved harder. It was no use. Then, from far away, an acrid smell assailed her senses. She turned her head back and forth, but she couldn't escape the choking, smothering fumes. The meadow faded around her, as if it were a movie screen losing its picture. And Catlin woke, gasping and coughing, struggling for air.

Smoke! The room was thick with smoke! She fought to get her bearings. Where was she? What was happening? "Fire!" She cried, suddenly fully awake

187

and afraid. "The room's on fire!" The smoke was so thick she couldn't see the edge of the bed. Her heart pumped and pounded, sending muscles into frenzied action.

Quickly she rolled off the bed and dropped onto her hands and knees, desperately gasping for the breathable air that hovered near the floor. She lay trembling for a few moments, filling her lungs with good air and struggled against wild, uncontrolled panic.

The door! She had to get to the door. Which way was it? She crawled, inch by inch in what she prayed was the correct direction. She couldn't see. The smoke blinded and stung her eyes. What if the fire was in the hallway? What if the doorknob was too hot to turn. Maybe the window would be better. But where would she go? From the window, it was a two-story drop to the ground! No, the hallway was her best course. A wet towel! Yes . . . she needed a wet towel.

She managed to get to the bathroom. Thankfully, the smoke had not filled this small room. Quickly she saturated a towel with water, wrung it out, and held it to her nose and mouth. Then she resumed her crawling toward the bedroom door.

Gingerly she reached up and jiggled the doorknob, her hand wrapped in the towel. The metal felt warm. That meant only one thing. The fire was in the hallway, too! Fighting a wave of terror, Catlin rose to her knees, holding the towel to her face, and tugged at the door.

It gave suddenly, swinging open against her. She saw thin, lapping yellow flames racing along the baseboards, toward the east end of the house. The flames seemed malicious, purposeful, as if they followed some secret passage . . . tiny bright soldiers, marching in a straight and determined path of destruction. She would have to cross over them to reach the banister that led to the staircase.

Catlin gathered her strength, stood, and jumped

through the trail of fire. She grasped the banister and clutched the wet towel, wrapping it around the singed hem of her gown, smothering out any sparks that might have found her. She lunged against the banister and stared down at the foyer below. The flames were behind her, racing along the wall, down the baseboard. Soon, they too, would reach the stairs, and her escape would be cut off.

"Matthew!" she screamed and stumbled along, gripping the banister railing, trying desperately to outdistance the rushing infantry of fire, but the flames reached the landing first, plunging along the wall, growing brighter and stronger with the fresh supply of oxygen. "Matthew!" She screamed again, forcing herself to go forward, hugging the banister rail, trying to meld into the wood spindles.

Catlin watched, mesmerized, as the greedy, consuming tongues of flame licked at the frame of Sandra's portrait, then moved across the canvas. The picture smoldered and flamed, dark holes of destruction spreading over the surface. . . . The fire absorbed, then devoured the beautiful image inbedded on the canvas.

"Catlin!" From the hypnotic haze of her trance, she heard someone calling her name. Like wind being sucked through a straw, the sound broke through to her consciousness.

Below her, at the base of the stairs, she saw Matthew. He called to her and she reached out for him, but the fire blocked her way. "Stay there!" he shouted. "I'll come get you!"

"No!" she screamed, realizing he would have to pass through the wall of fire. But it was too late. He was beside her instantly, lifting her, wrapping her in something. Then he ran back down the stairs, holding her in his arms. She ducked her head as they passed the remains of Sandra's portrait. They reached the marble foyer just as the painting fell with a roar, behind them.

Matthew carried her, gasping and choking into the frigid air. "Are you all right, baby?" he asked. "Oh, dear God . . . when I thought I couldn't reach you . . ." She lost the rest of his words as the roof on the east end of the house collapsed. She hid her face in Matthew's comforting arms, blotting out the inferno. He was here with her—her safety line in the madness around her. She was safe now. He and God would take care of her . . . .

And then Neal and Dodd were motioning them farther from the blazing house, and no one else spoke. They could only stand and watch as the fire did its work, snaking through the great mansion . . . consuming and destroying the fine old wood . . . engulfing and obliterating the antique furniture and heavy brocade drapes . . . melting the treasures of two hundred years . . . devouring the past in a vortex of fury.

Someone placed a coat across Catlin's shoulders and for the first time she realized she was cold—teeth-chattering, bone-chilling cold. All she heard was the roar and crackle of the flames. Then, from far away, she heard sirens screaming in the night, winding up through the dark hills. The firemen were coming, but they would be too late. The Newton-Van Cleef house—house of dreams and of an American dynasty—was gone forever.

The news cameras came, too. At least one crew got through the police barricade and onto the property. Catlin knew the routine. The media people—TV, radio, newspaper—would choose a pool team to cover the spectacle and ensure that everyone would get the story with the least risk of interruption to the firefighters.

From out of nowhere a TV reporter materialized and shoved a microphone in her face. "Catlin Burke!" The reporter eyed her suspiciously. "How did you get in here?" She was grateful for the cover of darkness and the overcoat hiding her nightgown.

Matthew turned to shield her with his body, to harbor her from the reporter's probing inquiries and the searching eye of his camera. "My house is burning!" he snapped. "This is hardly the time!"

"How did WTSB get here first?" the reporter persisted.

"I don't work for WTSB any more!" Catlin shouted above the chaos.

The newsman deliberated, torn between two stories, indecision reflected on his face. He glanced back at the house, then stepped closer to Matthew and Catlin. "What do you mean?" he yelled, as Matthew jerked open the door of a waiting car and pushed her inside.

"Ask Taylor Shentell!" she called out as Matthew slid in beside her and slammed the door behind him. Dodd gunned the motor and Neal rolled up the window, shutting out the night, the fire, the dumbstruck reporter.

Hours later, after all the firefighters had gone—the curious spectators, the campaign staff, the press—Catlin and Matthew stood gazing at the charred remains, still smoldering in the gray netherworld of predawn. The trees surrounding the house and lining the drive looked forlorn and lost, like guard dogs with no purpose.

Catlin inched closer to Matthew, hooked her arm through his, and stared at the ruins of the once-great house. It lay, broken and blackened, as if some giant had snapped it in halves and tossed it back to the earth—a heap of stones, smoking rubble, and melted glass.

"It's over," Matthew mused. "The Van Cleefs . . . their legacy . . . my stewardship." Phantoms from another time drifted away with the brightening of the approaching day. "In some ways, a burden has been lifted," he confessed. "And I'm free . . ."

The first pale streaks of dawn spread across the sky. Morning was breaking. New and crisp and fresh. Matthew turned to her and she slipped into his arms. He shook off his melancholy and gazed down at her lovingly.

"It's a brand-new day, Miss Burke," he said, a buoyant note in his voice. "In a couple of hours the polls will open. Let's go vote."

Suddenly Catlin felt joyous and carefree. Her spirits bubbled and her laughter spilled into the chilly, invigorating air. "Why, yes, Mr. Carr," she agreed. "I'm a woman of leisure now, as you know. I have no plans, no job to interfere with our day together."

His eyes twinkled in the swiftly gathering light. "Good!" he said. "I never wanted a working wife anyway."

Her heart pounded and she caught her breath. "Is that a proposal, Mr. Carr?" she asked coquettishly, afraid to exhale and risk banishing the magic and perfection of his words.

"It is. If you'll have me, that is. If I'm elected, we'll have to move to Washington immediately. Why, I don't even have a bed to share with you in this city." The intimate tone of his voice wrapped around her, and she rose on her toes and kissed him with sweet, promising abandon.

Matthew pulled back, cradled her face between his hands, and caressed her cheeks with his thumbs. His tone grew serious as he said, "It's the truth, Catlin. Everything I own—all my worldly goods—went up with that house."

She shrugged her shoulders and peered deep into his eyes. "A very wonderful man once told me that our forefathers got off their boats with little more than their Bibles. And they built a nation on that one foundation. *I* have one of those. . . ." She touched his face with the tip of her finger, trailing a line from his cheekbone to the corner of his mouth.

The sun broke above the horizon . . . a great, glowing ball, chasing away the remnants of the night and locking the two of them in its vermillion rays. "I also have a wedding quilt," she reminded him softly, ardently. "With those two things, I think we have a start. Don't you?"

He smiled. "Yes . . . we have a start, my love. The best start."

About the Author

Lurlene McDaniel has over one million books in print for the Young Adult market. Her series, *One Last Wish*, was recently launched by Bantam Books, following a string of successful titles dealing with teens facing life-threatening and life-altering events. Credited with carving out a new genre in the YA marketplace, Lurlene structures her works with a strong emphasis on Biblical values and ethics.

She is also Fiction Editor for *Faith 'n Stuff: The Magazine for Kids*, a Guideposts publication, and a frequent speaker and teacher at writing workshops and conferences. In the past, she has written numerous advertising, radio, and television commercials, as well as a magazine column.

Two of her novels were CBC/IRA Children's Choice Award winners, one has been awarded a RITA for Best YA of 1991 for Romance Writers of America, and one has been placed in a literary time capsule at the Library of Congress to be opened in 2089.

Lurlene has two grown sons and makes her home in Chattanooga, TN.